What did Tashi do?

Anangsha Alammyan

Ukiyoto Publishing

All global publishing rights are held by

Ukiyoto Publishing

Published in 2019

Content Copyright © **Anangsha Alammyan**
ISBN 9789359201146

All rights reserved.

No part of this publication may be reproduced, transmitted, or stored in a retrieval system, in any form by any means, electronic, mechanical, photocopying, recording or otherwise, without the prior permission of the publisher.

This is a work of fiction. Names, characters, businesses, places, events, locales, and incidents are either the products of the author's imagination or used in a fictitious manner. Any resemblance to actual persons, living or dead, or actual events is purely coincidental.

This book is sold subject to the condition that it shall not by way of trade or otherwise, be lent, resold, hired out or otherwise circulated, without the publisher's prior consent, in any form of binding or cover other than that in which it is published.

A spine-chilling tale of how a single mistake can pull you down the abyss of cybercrime

To all those who believe crime only happens in the movies: what if its next target is you?

This book is dedicated to the most talented person I know – the one who ideated this book with me and helped me get the technical details right -

Sai Krishna Kothapalli

CONTENTS

Prologue   1

Chapter One   3
You have five minutes. Tick tock.

Chapter Two   12
One click and you're done

Chapter Three   23
I am right beside you

Chapter Four   32
The gods must have been laughing

Chapter Five   44
But he was my best friend

Chapter Six   52
The only way out of this mess

Chapter Seven   72
Tashi, you crazy woman

Chapter Eight   84
It is a dead end

Chapter Nine   101
Just some drunk men

Chapter Ten   120
Blackcurrant or chocolate?

Epilogue: And After   125

About the Author   *130*
Note From The Author   *131*

Prologue

The man scrolled through the photographs he had saved in his protected folder. It disappointed him slightly; he had seen them all and used them to his heart's content.

He needed more, and he needed them soon.

He remembered the woman's name well. All he had to do was check her Instagram profile. He typed her name in the search bar and pressed enter. When he saw the first thumbnail among the search results, a primal excitement spread in his loins.

It was her. And her profile was public.

Greed and anticipation making his heart beat faster, he went through the selfies, sunsets, and quotes till he came across a photograph she had uploaded seven weeks back. It was a no-make-up selfie of the woman with her mother. "Chilling at home with mom," the caption read.

What interested the man the most was the location along with the caption. He clicked on the map link and opened a photographic view of her street: he noted she lived in a twelve-story apartment.

"Sweet," he thought, as he cleared his search history and got ready to leave. He had had enough of playing the game on his computer.

Things were about to get real now.

Chapter One

You have five minutes. Tick tock.

It was eleven in the night.

A lone dog greeted the cab that stopped in front of a twelve-storeyed apartment with a low howl. A slender young woman got down, glancing at the deserted street for a moment before turning to pay the driver. Heels rapping smartly on the concrete, she looked at her watch and waited for him to return the change.

She was a little over five feet tall, dressed in fitted black trousers and a matching blazer. A large shoulder bag was slung to her right, blocking half her body from vision, failing, however, to hide the alluring shape of her chest. Her thick black hair highlighted with a bold auburn shade fell to her shoulders in cascades, casting shadows on her pale face. Her full lips were painted red and the epicanthic folds in her eyes were rimmed in black kohl. The woman's name was Tashi Chotten and today had been her first work anniversary as a graduate trainee engineer at a reputed EPC firm in New Delhi.

Tashi walked inside the building and pressed the button on the elevator for the tenth floor. When the doors slid open in front of her flat, she noted that the lights were out. Her mother must have fallen asleep, she realised. With a twinge of guilt, Tashi remembered that her mother had been insisting for over a week that the two of them should have at least one meal in the day together. But with the current project going on in full swing and a purported promotion around the corner, she had been unable to find time for that.

Holding her own as a woman from Arunachal Pradesh amid the cut-throat competition in the country's capital hadn't been a cakewalk, and Tashi had been alone through most of her journey. Only recently, she had saved enough to bring her mother to stay with her from their village back in Bomdila. Her mother was the only family Tashi had, and it brightened her days after they lived together. Her little apartment felt more like home. Tashi turned the key in the lock and said to herself for the fourth time that week – 'Tomorrow I'm coming home early.'

She entered the house and fumbled on the adjacent wall to turn on the lights. In the darkness, her right knee caught against a table below the switches. "Fuck," she exclaimed in frustration. She bent to rub her knee with her right hand as she turned on the lights with her left. The familiar living room and the kitchen came into view. She straightened and walked towards her bedroom.

Tashi entered the comfort of her room and hung her blazer neatly by the door. She then took out her laptop and tossed her bag on the couch. She let out a soft moan as she took off her shoes after a long day of walking in heels. She turned to her wardrobe and hummed as she undressed and changed into her nightgown. It was a silk negligee that fell to her knees: black, with silver flowers printed all over - a lavish present to herself she had purchased on a whim a few days back. She took a moment to revel in the comfort of the soft fabric hugging her skin and then walked back into the kitchen to see what her mother had prepared for dinner.

She uncovered the plastic bowls inside the refrigerator and saw it was rice and chicken stew. Tashi put the chicken inside the microwave oven to heat it up and walked over to the kitchen sink to wash her hands. As she worked up a lather, she bit her lips, lost in thought, trying to remember the lyrics of the song that had been playing in her cab while returning home. The tune was stuck in her head, but she couldn't quite place the words. The ping of the microwave oven brought her back to reality, and she turned around, wiping her hands on a paper towel. She laid out her dinner carefully on a dish and carried it back to her bedroom. Then she lay on her tummy, with the plate beside her laptop and put a chunky chicken piece in her mouth with a fork. Tashi couldn't help smiling when she thought about how mad her mother would have been, had she seen her having her meal in bed. "How many times should I tell you to only have meals on the dining table?" she would have scolded, an adorable look of exasperation on her face.

Tashi turned on her computer and opened a Facebook tab. Her feed was filled with photographs of her friends either getting married, going on honeymoons and throwing baby showers, or getting promotions, switching to higher-paying jobs and moving abroad for further studies. It seemed as if all of them had their entire lives planned out while here she was, not sure if she could squeeze in a few hours during the weekend to spend time with her mother.

Sighing, she opened another tab to look through her emails. Ignoring the updates from work and a couple of advertisements promising dirt-cheap weekend getaways, an email from an unfamiliar sender caught her attention. "Important," the subject read. It had a photo attached.

Curious, she clicked on the attachment.

When the image loaded onto the screen, Tashi's mouth hung open in shock – it was her own photograph: pouting with full lips at the camera, dressed in nothing but a lacy black bra and matching panties.

She gaped at the screen, eyes wide with disbelief. No, this can't be happening, she thought furiously. Her heart was pounding, her mouth suddenly dry.

At a loss for what to do, she refreshed the page, hoping that somehow it would disappear and she would realise she had been daydreaming.

The page loaded. The image on the screen stayed resolutely the same.

Head reeling with disbelief, Tashi read frantically through the accompanying text. There were only three lines, but she read them over and over again till her brain fuddled up and stopped trying to make sense of the words.

I have access to all your pictures.

I'll keep this a secret between us if you do whatever I tell you to.

I'll start simple: Send me a picture of what you're wearing right now.

It was not possible. Her brain went into overdrive trying to connect the dots as to who might be behind this.

Akash is the only person whom I'd sent that photograph – that too four years back, she thought. Is he trying to get back at me?

A million emotions raced in her head; confusion and denial flaring the brightest, obscuring all else. With trembling fingers, she searched anxiously through her contacts and dialled Akash's number. It rang for a full minute but he didn't pick up. She slammed the phone on the bed and instinctively bit her nails.

Tashi was terrified. She didn't know what else to do, so she called her ex-boyfriend up again. This time, a voice groggy with sleep answered. "Hello?"

She was trying hard not to hyperventilate. "Akash, it's me." The surprised intake of breath on the other end told her he still recognized her voice.

She started off without preamble – "How dare you send me that email?"

"Wait, what? What email?" his voice registered confusion.

"Those pictures of mine I had sent when we were together," she almost sobbed.

"Why would I send you pictures?" he asked, his voice raised in anger at her accusing tone.

"I got an email with a – an explicit picture from our time together – and the mail. Oh God, Akash, it is threatening horrible stuff," she cried.

"What? Am I there in the picture too?"

"No, it is one of those selfies I clicked for you in front of the mirror."

"This is bad," he said, thinking fast. "Did they ask for money?"

"No. But they asked me to share more pictures."

His sigh of relief was almost audible. "Whatever you do, do not share any more pictures. We don't know what is going on."

"Tell me Akash," she continued. "What the fuck did you do? If you claim you're not the one behind this, then did you share those pictures with anyone else?"

"Tashi, I have no clue what you are talking about," he said.

"How do I believe it when you're the only person who had access to them?" she shouted.

"If what you're saying is true, then either your account has been hacked or somebody else has had access to your computer. You should get in touch with the police at once."

She got distracted by the notification for a new email flashing on her computer screen. It was from the same sender.

The police might find me, but they will take at least a week. Imagine the damage I can do in that time. For starters, I will upload this picture on Facebook and tag you - so that all your friends and family members can see it. I think you look smoking hot. Sexy, wouldn't you say?

If you don't want that to happen, do as I tell you. You have five minutes to send a picture of what you are wearing. Tick tock.

Her heart thumping against her chest, she hung up on Akash and stared at the screen. She felt helpless- with no clue what to do next.

Her dinner lay forgotten on the bed – the microwaved chicken gone cold.

A fresh bout of tears blurred her vision. It made her mascara run down her deathly white face in black rivulets of fear and shame.

Chapter Two

One click and you're done

A ray of sunlight broke through the mullioned window and cast a checkerboard of brilliant morning light across Tashi's bed. She raised a hand to cover her face, eyelids fluttering for a while, then opening. She sat up and stretched her arms, taking in the familiar sounds of the cooing pigeons nesting above her window. For a moment, she couldn't quite place the strange heaviness in her heart. She blinked several times to clear the veil of slumber from her eyes. Slowly, bits and pieces of the happenings of the previous night came back.

She had gone to bed late last night, and in her sleep-deprived state, she allowed herself a small hope that maybe all of last night was a bad dream, the product of her paranoia.

She held her breath and checked her phone. The last email on it was *"If you don't listen to what I tell you, I'll mail your naked pictures to everyone who is even remotely connected to you professionally. I'll destroy your career."*

The world around her faded to that tiny rectangle of her screen, alive with the gleaming reflection of the inferno of fear blazing in her eyes. The walls of the room felt like they were closing in – blurring her vision, leaving her no room to breathe.

In a gush, all the terrible memories came back. She sobbed, arms wrapped tightly around her shivering body.

There was nowhere to go — no place to hide her shame. She curled up in bed and faced the wall.

What was happening to her? How could she make it stop?

She took a breath. *"Who the fuck are you?"* she typed, pulling out the faintest wisps of courage and weaving them around her conscience like a shield. *"I am not letting you blackmail me; do you get it? Do whatever you wish, but I swear I'm going to see you behind bars."*

She sent the message on an impulse, but the words sounded braver than she felt.

She took her phone and desperately looked up ways online to see if there was something she could do to ask for help in a situation like this without compromising her dignity.

Within seconds of sending her reply, she had another new email waiting. *"If you try to contact the Police, I will bring you down with me. I might be behind bars, but the entire world would know what a shameless slut the innocent-looking Tashi Chotten is."*

She felt disgusted by his choice of words. Who was he to make comments about her body, about the choices she had made in the past? What gave him the right to call her a slut when he himself hid conveniently behind the mask of anonymity? Anger bubbling on the surface of her emotions, she typed. *"Fuck you. You can't do anything so extreme with just one picture. You're bluffing – I know you have nothing more on me."*

His reply made her shiver. *"If you want to take chances, first see how high the stakes are."*

Attached to the message, was a screenshot showing the thumbnails of several pictures of herself in different phases of her life – half-dressed or naked, always throwing a lusty look at the camera. There was a thumbnail of a video where she had two fingers between her legs. Tashi gulped. She remembered how the video ended – her masturbating furiously to an intense orgasm, moaning Akash's name out loud. The other thumbnail was of a video of Akash fucking her while she lay on the bed, legs spread wide. She remembered this one too – how she had moaned and begged for him to go harder; and how, after an intense session of panting and grunting, he had pulled out and spilled his load on her belly. Akash's face wasn't visible as he was the one holding the camera while recording the video. But Tashi's flushed face, her bouncing breasts and the curve of her waist and belly could be seen clearly throughout.

It was a screenshot of all the raunchy footage she had recorded when she was young, naïve, and blindly in love with Akash.

Something happened inside her mind. It was physical. She could feel as if large glass windows were shattering in the centre of her brain, and try as she might, she couldn't stop the pain.

The thought that someone else had seen something so personal made her feel sick to the stomach. Her body felt like it was on fire and drenched in ice-cold water at the same time.

She screamed out in rage.

Just then, there was a sharp rap on her door.

She sat up, her heart beating fast.

It was only her mother. "Ashi dear, you woke up late today. I am happy that after so long we can have breakfast together. I have prepared duck-egg omelettes – for you. Get dressed and come out so we can eat before you leave for office."

She took a few breaths to calm herself. "Mom," she called out. "I'm working from home today – there is a lot of stuff for me to get done, so I'll be busy all day. Don't disturb me, I'm not hungry."

Her mother sounded hurt when she said, "But dear, at least have some milk? It is bad for your health to work on an empty stomach."

"Mom, leave me alone," she said, exasperated. "I have lots of work."

She heard a sharp intake of breath from outside and the sound of sandalled feet walking away. Tashi felt bad as she realised she had lost patience and shouted at her mother for no fault of hers. In her attempt to hide her trauma from the world, she had hurt the one person who considered having a meal with her daughter the highlight of her day.

She fell back on the bed, a fresh wave of sobs assailing her.

Looking at the screenshot through a veil of tears, Tashi realised how trapped she was - as if nothing she said or did would make any difference. But this was her shame – her punishment. Her mother didn't deserve this uncalled for rudeness.

Gritting her teeth, she decided she would do anything to shield her mother from the humiliation of it all.

But with the blackmailer having access to so much of her dark secrets, she couldn't see a way out.

In a flash, multiple scenarios played in her head. What if her uncles found out? After her father had passed away when she was but a child, her mother's brothers had helped raise her. Though on the face of it the family appeared content, Tashi had lost count of the nights she had gone to bed with an empty stomach, too sad to eat because of the harsh words of insult they had rained on her mother. They shamed her for being a widow, always questioning her decision of not remarrying and raising her daughter as a single parent. Oh, how pleased they would be when they found out the shame this daughter had brought upon her.

What if her colleagues saw these pictures? She couldn't bear to imagine the trauma their looks of judgment would put her through. If these images were made public, would she be able to work anywhere again?

Would she be able to face the society with her head held high?

Bitterly, she realised the answer to all these questions was 'no'. It would destroy her life when the world saw the images.

Shuddering at the thought, Tashi corrected herself – *if* the world saw, not *when*.

She wouldn't let this be public. She would do whatever she could to appease the blackmailer so her reputation wouldn't be damaged.

She picked up her phone and scrolled through the mails she had exchanged with the blackmailer since last night. *"Show me a picture of what you're wearing,"* was his recurring demand.

Tashi turned on the camera on her phone and clicked a selfie of herself without showing her face – focussing only on the swell of her chest covered by the flowery nightgown she was wearing.

She held her breath and clicked 'send'.

For a few hours hence, she received no new emails. She relaxed and stepped out of her room when she was called for lunch. Her mother was happily chatting away at how they could talk after so long, but Tashi could barely take part in the conversation. Her mind was in a whirl, replaying the events that had transpired since last night.

She was at a loss for how the blackmailer had gained access to her pictures. All traces of Akash had been deleted from her online presence back in college itself. She had made him swear on his mother that he too would delete all the incriminating evidence. Nevertheless, the only way these pictures could have been accessed was if he was behind this somehow. She wanted to confront him again, but his confusion last night at her accusations had sounded genuine. She didn't dare approach the police because she had no experience in these matters and her opinion about them wasn't positive. In fact, after her father had his accident when she was but a child, the police had harassed her mother for a long time before releasing his body for funeral rites. Also, what if the blackmailer was caught, but couldn't be imprisoned because of lack of evidence? Wouldn't he make her life worse?

Defeated, Tashi struggled through lunch and asked her mother to not make dinner for her as she was tired and would sleep early. When her mother refused to budge, she almost yelled, "Nothing will happen if I don't have dinner for one day, okay? Please let me be."

She shut the door on her mother's crestfallen face and locked herself from inside.

Lying to people who trust you has become so easy, she thought with regret.

***

For the rest of the evening, Tashi had just lain on her bed. Not sleeping, but wishing she could. Thinking, but wishing she would stop. Not crying... but somehow wishing she could. She had drawn all the blinds shut, making her room as dark as her mood.

She had calmed the blackmailer down for the time being, it seemed, for he hadn't contacted her after she had sent that selfie.

She turned on her laptop to get her mind off the present. Almost instantly, the screen pinged with a new email.

Anxious, she clicked on the attached image. It was a screenshot of an email draft addressed to all the employees of the company she worked in. Seven of her naked pictures were attached – it seemed the blackmailer had taken pleasure in selecting the raunchiest, most embarrassing photographs. Tashi cringed and closed her eyes, blinking back tears. The subject read **"Sluttiest employee of the month award goes to..."**

The mouse pointer was hovering threateningly over the "send" button.

"Just one click and you're done," read the accompanying text. *"If I don't have a full-frontal nude of yours within five minutes, I will hit send."*

Her breath caught in her throat.

She looked away from the screen, filled with terror. There were hot tears of shame running down her face. All her facade of having kept him satisfied with the selfie earlier came crashing down. *This time, the consequences are real;* she thought. *This time, I cannot get away from him.*

She felt violated, bitter at the thought of being used for somebody else's perverted pleasure.

Her heart was pounding violently against her chest. It was as if wave after wave of fear assailed her entire being and her stomach fell flat to the floor. There was a sharp pain shooting down her legs. She got so afraid that she sat down on the bed and took several deep breaths to calm herself.

The whirring of the fan above was uncomfortably loud in her ears - she shut them with both her hands and screamed in frustration, tears running down both her cheeks.

The time on the phone caught her attention. She had only two minutes left.

Tashi felt cold, as if she had ice running through her veins instead of blood. With trembling hands, she fumbled to undo the clasp of her dress at the back.

In a single, fluid motion, her nightgown fell down. It settled around her legs in a crumpled mess, leaving Tashi naked.

Exposed.

Chapter Three

I am right beside you

It was a chilly Sunday afternoon, almost three weeks after that first email.

Tashi stepped out of her home to do some grocery shopping. She had wanted nothing better than to curl up in bed and introspect, but her mother had forced her out of her room to talk with her. She was concerned about her state of mind, why she kept refusing meals and why she hardly shared anything about her day anymore. Tashi dodged all questions, not wanting to burden her mother. After several failed attempts at proposing an outing, she had reluctantly agreed to go out and buy some milk.

But Tashi regretted her decision almost instantly. The weak sun felt harsh on her face and seeing so many people milling around filled her with inexplicable anxiety. Her otherwise lustrous hair hung around her face in lank, oily strands. The deep brown rings rimming her eyes and the tired lines around her mouth were telling of having spent several sleepless nights on end. Her crumpled brown jacket and black jeans hung loosely on her frail frame.

A storm of chaotic emotions was raging on inside her head. Throughout the past three weeks, she had, more or less, figured out a rhythm - a routine - for the blackmailer. He sent her emails mostly at night, at an interval of two or three days. Some times, he was content with taunting her and calling her a whore for having sex with a man she had no intention of marrying. He seemed to derive a sadistic pleasure from shaming her for having a high libido. But on others, he got more demanding and wanted her to send naked pictures. Out of hopelessness, she had obliged but had hidden her face or blurred her features despite his persistent requests. There were some nights, however, when he made outrageous demands. His messages were riddled with spelling mistakes on those nights – almost as if he were drunk. She had come to discover that the best way out of these situations was to calm him down in whichever way she could, so he didn't end up doing something extreme in his inebriated state.

She felt a little light-hearted on the days she calculated he wouldn't contact her. It was easier going about her life without the sustained fear of looking at her phone and discovering something traumatic nagging at her. Even then, she was constantly on the edge, jumping every time her phone pinged with a new notification.

That an anonymous person on the internet held so much power over her life made her feel helpless; that he could use words and pictures to make her feel disgusted about her own body filled her with shame and fear.

Her social life had taken a heavy toll; she refused to meet her friends when they came knocking at her door on weekends. Her mother had invented so many new stories each time to send them away, that she was afraid she might run out of excuses soon. Her colleagues had remarked on her lack of enthusiasm several times, but she had plastered a fake smile on her face till they gave up and moved on to the next topic of discussion.

On the surface, Tashi was content being alone.

But in truth, she felt lonelier than ever. It was difficult digesting the fact that all her friends were so 'normal' – that they spent hours obsessing over such trivial issues like rising petrol prices or unavailability of movie tickets for the evening show, while she, on the other hand, had such a complex situation to deal with. In the inky shell of her desolation, Tashi was alienated from the rest of the world.

No wonder she kept pushing even her closest friends away.

***

The sun pushed meekly through a curtain of clouds, the weak sunlight unsuccessful in lighting up the gloomy Sunday afternoon.

Tashi walked on, shuddering as she remembered what had transpired last night – her blackmailer had demanded something that had knotted her heart into a horrible, tight mess.

"I want to see you strip for me, bitch."

It was one of those nights - his email was riddled with spelling mistakes: Tashi figured he must be intoxicated.

"In five minutes, you are going to get a video call from me. You will remove ALL your clothes one by one till you are naked. And this time, I want to look at your face when you do it."

Her skin crawled at the humiliation he was subjecting her to.

Her knee-jerk reaction was to refuse. *"Fuck off,"* she typed. *"I am not doing anything like that."*

"You don't get to decide that," came his reply. *"I am the one doing the talking, and when I wag my tongue, you will wag your fingers between your legs. I want to make you cum with my words. I know how much you will enjoy that, you slut."*

His remarks disgusted her. *"No. Absolutely not,"* she typed. *"There is no way I am getting on a video call, you perverted asshole."*

She had closed her laptop in a huff, turned off her phone and stared into the darkness. Her chest was heaving, her breath coming in gasps. Her heart was thumping so hard, she could feel the blood pounding in her ears.

Refusing to oblige him had been an impulsive decision. She went to bed in a fit of denial.

This recklessness of those two seconds, however, couldn't calm the tempest of uncertainty in her soul. She kept picturing what would happen to her if he resorted to taking drastic measures. The thought of the impact her leaked images would have on her reputation at her workplace and that of her mother in front of her extended family had kept her up all night in abject fear.

This morning, she had turned on her phone to no new email from him. Seeing an empty inbox was relieving. This was the first time in three weeks she had so boldly defied him. She allowed herself some hope that maybe he had given up on her after the courage she had shown last night. It was hard, though, to let go of the constant fear plaguing her thoughts: *what if this is the calm before the storm? What if he acts on his threats and does something irreversible to make me pay for last night?* Her instinct was screaming inside her head: *why do I feel unsafe stepping out of the comfort of my house?*

Pulling her jacket tighter around herself, Tashi brushed off the irrational fear she felt. She only had to go to a departmental store a few blocks away. *There is nothing he can do that he hasn't already done,* she kept telling herself.

The sudden vibration of her phone sent jitters through her body.

She was terrified at the prospect of interacting with her tormentor again – listening to another jibe, feeling violated at him taking more perverted pleasure in her plight. With an icy fist clutched around her heart, she took the phone out of her bag. She held her breath as she looked at the screen - it was a call from her mother.

She let out an audible sigh of relief.

"Ashi dear, I'd forgotten to tell you I need some hair colour too. Can you get a packet for me?"

"Yes Mom, sure thing. I'm on my way to the store."

"Okay, I'll text if anything else comes up. See you."

"Bye Mom."

The comfort in the familiarity of her voice helped bring Tashi's thumping heart back to normal. She walked onwards again. Perhaps, after last night, the blackmailer had given up.

Perhaps, things would be all right again.

Little by little, Tashi felt the tension draining from her body.

Her phone beeped again with a new message. *Mum must have remembered something else,* she thought with a slight smile. When she looked at the screen, her heart sank. It was a text message from an unknown number. She didn't have to open it to know it was from the blackmailer.

"Did you think you are free? I will show you that whatever you do is under my control."

Attached with it was a picture of hers – clicked a few moments ago, dressed in her crumpled brown jacket and black jeans, standing with back against the handrail and talking on the phone.

"Do you know how close I am to you right now?"

The world seemed to have stopped.

In slow motion, Tashi turned around.

This can't be happening, she thought, fighting to reason with her senses screaming for an escape.

She was terrified, half expecting to see someone smirking at her.

This is my place, my locality. He isn't supposed to be here.

Everyone she saw seemed to stare at her, cold judgement in their eyes. She felt as if they knew her secret - that every one of them had seen her naked.

She turned violently, specks of sweat flying in the air. There was an old lady sitting on a bench, knitting a sweater with light pink wool. There were two young women at a roadside store, shielding their cigarettes from wind as they lit them with a single match. A man walked by her, his hand clasped around the fingers of a little girl in a red frock. The child looked up at Tashi as they passed by, her big round eyes fixing on her with a searching look. Tashi rummaged through the sea of faces, her black hair astray, looking for any telltale signs that one of them might be her blackmailer. But all she could see was the crowd milling around, caught up in their own worlds. The faces were devoid of emotion, but when they turned towards her, she could feel them sparing enough contempt to cast a disdainful glance.

Tashi ran her tongue around the inside of her mouth, which had gone dry under the scrutiny of the strangers. Fear welled up inside her like a shoal of fish uncurling from sleep and swimming out in formation in a primordial sea. Then, too scared to be standing among so many people, she spun around and ran, all thoughts of shopping forgotten.

She didn't know where to go, which turn to take.

She didn't know where she might feel *safe*.

Chapter Four

The gods must have been laughing

It was raining outside.

Frail arms closed about her drawn-up knees, head lowered, sheathed in limp hair that hadn't been washed in days, Tashi wept. Her sobbing helped her withdraw into herself, to seek solace in a place deep within that was unrelenting and unforgiving.

Her phone lay forgotten by her side, the screen flashing with four unread emails from the blackmailer.

Over the past three weeks, her tormentor had kept her constantly on the edge, but today – with a single text message showing her just how close by he was, he had shaken her entire world. The thin line that blurred her reality from the horror online was shattered, and she had no hope of turning back.

This thought felt heavy as a sack full of rocks on her frail heart.

Unbidden, her mind conjured up a memory of Akash's trembling voice on the phone. He had been bold in suggesting they go to the police, but he hadn't contacted her during the next few days. She was convinced that he wasn't the one blackmailing her, but after what had transpired today, she knew she could no longer be sure of anything.

Akash didn't know her current address. But he had friends who did, and it wouldn't be difficult for him to turn up at her doorstep to intimidate her if he wanted to.

She shook off the thought, as a fresh wave of shivers racked her body. She let her mind dredge up memories of the past – a visage of the days she had purposefully locked away in the viscid pools of her consciousness.

She remembered Akash's face, his dark hair that was straight on most days, curly on some; how she had loved running her fingers through it, how she had joked it would never be fully straight. She thought of his lean frame, and though, since their breakup, it had been impossible to think of Akash without feeling resentment; she recognised a faint twinge of fondness as she recalled how safe his embrace had made her feel. She thought of the stubble on his face, and how often he had whined that he would look like a teenager if he shaved it off.

Helpless and with no one to turn to, Tashi found herself reliving the reason she had given up on what she had hoped would be a future filled with promise.

It had been raining heavily that night - just like today. She had told Akash her period was two weeks late. "What would you do if I were pregnant?" she had joked. Akash was worried sick about it and had gotten her a pregnancy test kit. She was laughing with him on the phone when she took the test – joking it was impossible that their protection had failed, that they had been careful each time.

Careful? The gods must have been laughing, Tashi thought bitterly.

She remembered how her heart had jumped to her throat when the pink patch on the test strip had kept moving upwards after showing the first line – how it had climbed steadily ahead to settle at two pink lines – clear and distinct. The confusion in her head had changed instantly to shock.

Then, to denial.

They were barely twenty-two then, struggling with their studies, with no clue what they would make of their lives.

She had screamed on the phone – "Fuck, I'm pregnant".

"What? No! How can that be possible?" Akash had begged for an answer.

"I have no fucking clue."

"This has to be fixed. You have to get rid of the baby at once."

"Of course, we will do it together."

"Yes, yes. It's a big headache. I want you to go to a doctor tomorrow and confirm this. Ask him how to kill it the soonest."

"You will not come?"

"Um, I wish I could. But I have an exam until 5 PM. You visit the doctor. Let me know what he said."

"You don't want to be there with me? Fine!" she said and hung up.

She had feigned anger, hoping he would calm her down; that he would apologise for his behaviour and offer to accompany her to the hospital.

She sat by the window for a long time after that, waiting for him to call back and set things straight.

Her phone never rang.

***

The next day, she went to the hospital unaccompanied.

The gynaecologist had confirmed she was six weeks pregnant. Citing possible future complications, he had urged her to get her pregnancy terminated the next day itself. When she called Akash up and told him everything, he instantly agreed.

On the next day, only an hour before the doctor's appointment, the two of them were sitting in the college cafeteria discussing the course of action. Akash was dressed in a blue tee and black jeans; his hair was straight that day. Tashi moved from across the table to sit next to him and hold his hand, when he got a call. It was from his friend, Ravi, saying the recruitment interview of one of his dream companies that day.

After he had hung up, Akash bit his lower lip and looked at her with regret in his eyes. "I really wish I could go, but I can't miss this interview.

Can we reschedule the procedure for tomorrow?" he had asked.

"But I have fasted since last night and already taken the prescribed pre-abortion pills."

"Uh so this means-"

"There is no way I can postpone. We have to do this today, Akash," she had pleaded.

He looked dejected. "You are brave, Tashu. I know you can do it without me," he had given her a sad smile offered to walk with her to her hostel room before she could pack some clothes and leave for the hospital.

Tashi was in shock all the way. The moment he left, she lost it. She felt to the floor of her room, breaking down in helpless, uncontrollable sobs. She didn't know how she could go through this on her own, and in her desperation, had called up her best friend Manav.

She was breathless with sobs when he answered her call. She asked him if he could go with her to the hospital. He agreed instantly without asking her why. Within minutes, he had booked an auto-rickshaw and arrived at her hostel gate to pick her up. On their way to the hospital, she told him the full story. Manav nodded and put an arm round her shoulder as if to shield her from the atrocities of the world.

Hours later, she was lying unconscious on a cold bed, with metal spoons being inserted into her womb to scoop out the life growing within her. Manav had been there through it all – rushing to the nearby medical stores to get medicines when the doctors prescribed something new. After she woke up from her anaesthesia-induced unconsciousness, she shivered and cried for Akash.

But he wasn't around.

It was Manav who put an extra blanket around her and held her hand till her grogginess subsided. Tashi had suffered from a bout of debilitating depression for several days after. She stopped attending classes and going about her daily routine. All she could obsess over was the baby she had just murdered. Whenever she tried to force herself to focus on something else, her thoughts inadvertently returned to that hospital bed and the look on the face of the doctor when he told her she was no longer pregnant. Her friends and classmates kept going on about life as usual, and many of them stopped to ask her if she was all right. She faked a smile, assuring them that everything was fine, that she was only feeling under the weather. Only in her heart, she knew how much she longed for Akash's company and support. The two of them had survived a fierce whirlpool of emotions, and he was the only one who could truly understand what she was going through. She wanted him close by.

But Akash was resolutely in denial throughout.

Manav had been her sole support in that dark phase. Though his ways of trying to make her laugh didn't always work – in the end, he brought the old happy-go-lucky Tashi back.

Apparently, he had supported her a bit too much.

Because right after she had recovered from the post-operation bleeding and stomach cramps, Akash had taken her out on a date to their favourite park. Tashi still remembered the day like it was yesterday. Akash had worn her favourite red shirt with black stripes, and his hair had set itself to an adorably curly mane. He fed her ice cream and asked her in a serious tone: "You and Manav seem to have grown," he cleared his throat, "close these days."

His emphasis on the word "close" caught her attention. She stared at him, not sure what to expect.

"All my friends have been saying," Akash continued, fumbling with his watch, refusing to meet her eyes, "that from the beginning of this semester, you have been spending more time with him than you did with me."

"May I ask which friend of yours said this?" she said contemptuously.

"Ravi did. But does it matter?" He looked down again. "I have a question, Tashi."

She waited, arms crossed, her foot tapping impatiently on the sidewalk. She felt as though she was on the edge; that all that was needed for everything to go berserk was one push.

"The baby you just killed, are you sure it didn't belong to Manav?"

She could only stare, as the world around came crumpling down.

This man, the one for whom she had nurtured so much love that she hadn't even blamed him for his callousness during the abortion, had the audacity to suggest that she had cheated on him. A mad rage was boiling in her heart, but it manifested itself in hot tears streaking her flushed cheeks. "How could you?" she spoke quietly, her voice trembling with anger. "After everything I did for you, how could you allege this?"

She threw her bag to the ground in a huff and walked away.

"Wait, Tashi. Tashi!" Akash had called out. He picked her bag up and ran after her.

Tashi didn't heed his pleas.

That had been the deal breaker – the last straw that sealed the relationship in her eyes. He had come round a few hours later, calling her incessantly and begging for forgiveness, but she had turned a deaf ear to his cries.

How could she be with a man who didn't have an iota of respect for her?

Months passed and the day of their graduation drew close. Tashi had blocked Akash on every social media platform. She had taken to turning in the opposite direction every time she spotted him in the corridors. It was hard for her - the decision to break up with Akash had torn her apart. But she couldn't just stop loving him because he hurt her, although things would have been easier if she could. She tried her best, though, to erase Akash from her conversations, the same way she had erased him from her memory - not without pain, but thoroughly.

On their last day in college, he had cornered her when she was least expecting it. Looking dapper in a fitted blue suit, with his hair sleeked up with gel, Akash had gone down on his knees, head hung in shame. There were tears in his eyes when he said how sorry he was, and how he would consider himself lucky if she forgave him.

Tashi didn't want to create a scene in front of their classmates who had gathered around them. She agreed to part without any hard feelings. They shook hands as their friends cheered and hooted. When the crowd had cleared, Akash held her elbow, pulled her aside and asked, "There is no turning back, is there?"

"Even if we could turn back, do you think we would end up where we started?" she asked drily. Akash stared at her for a while. Then, he shook his head slowly and turned away without a word. That was the last she had seen of him.

After college, they hadn't kept in touch – until one night a few months back when she assumed he had drunk-dialled her number. It was almost 2 AM, and she had woken up in confusion by the incessant ringing of her phone. She stared at his name on the screen for a full minute, her heart racing, before keeping the phone on silent and going back to sleep. She answered none of his twenty of so calls that night, and he hadn't called back to follow up the next day.

This isolated incident was the only reminder that Akash still existed in her life. This, and that terrible day three weeks back when she had called him up to hurl accusations at him in her desperate state of mind.

The shrill ring of her phone broke the stillness of the night into a million shards. Startled out of her thoughts, Tashi turned violently and picked up her phone, expecting the worst.

It wasn't an unknown number. It wasn't her mother either.

It was Akash.

Hands quivering, she put the phone to her ears and in a trembling voice, said, "Hello?"

"Tashi, I have something terrible to confess," came Akash's voice from the other end.

He had been crying.

Chapter Five

But he was my best friend

Tashi sat up straight, not sure of what to expect.

"Do you remember my friend Ravi from section B?"

"Yes, Ravikant, your so-called best friend. I could never bring myself to like him - he made me uncomfortable at times."

"He and I were friends from the first year. You know how close we were. So, um, after you broke up with me, Ravi – sort of – asked me for your nudes sometimes."

Tashi was horrified. "What? Don't tell me you obliged?"

"No, I never let him save your pictures, I swear," his voice sounded more uncomfortable now. "But there were times when I... uh, when I *showed* him some of them."

She was disgusted. "How could you have done that? I trusted you so much, I never -"

"Calm down, Tashu," he said using the name he had called her all those years back. "I was an asshole and I accept it. This is something I am extremely ashamed of, and I - I swear, if there was a way I could undo it, I would. But right now, you need to stay calm and listen to me."

Tashi waited, her face set in anger. Akash had made all her memories of the relationship feel like a sham in retrospect. She wanted to hit him on the head with something heavy.

"When you called me up the other night, I was terrified that somehow Ravi was connected with the blackmailing. I was so angry, I drove straight to his apartment and confronted him. He was nearly driven to tears trying to convince me he had never saved a single picture of yours. I know he can be an asshole, Tashi, but to people who knew him well, he had always been a terrible liar. I believe him – he doesn't have a hand in this."

"Fuck you, Akash. Apart from Ravikant, how many others have you shown my pictures to?"

"There is nobody else, I swear. I only showed a couple to Ravi – that too when he got really insistent."

"Insistent? I don't believe this! Didn't you have the slightest bit of respect for me?"

"Always, Tashi. I always respected you. It's just that I was young and heartbroken back then. There were times when I wanted to pull my hair out and scream at you for leaving me like that. But you weren't even speaking to me. It was hard to figure out – I hated myself for letting you down, but I wanted to get back at you for making me feel that way. I'm not defending myself, but those days I felt helpless and the only way I could vent my anger was by indulging Ravi's wishes."

It sounded like he was crying again. She scoffed. "At least tell me you have deleted those photographs now?"

The silence on the other end was punctuated by his sniffs.

"You still have them?" she yelled.

"Tashi, I -"

"I knew you're an asshole, but I couldn't have believed you would stoop to such levels. I am ashamed I had anything to do with you."

"Tashi, please. I deleted them the night you called me. I –"

"After everything you told me, do you still expect me to believe you had nothing to do with the blackmailing? Do I look like a fucking retard to you?" she shouted.

"Tashi, I-"

"I am going to the Police straight away. Make sure you hire a good lawyer because I promise I am not letting you get off easy."

She hung up and tossed her phone aside in anger. She held her head in her hands, her long, black hair falling over her flushed face. She picked a bottle from her bedside table, poured herself a glass of water and emptied it with loud gulps. Her blood was boiling with rage, but somewhere deep inside, she felt betrayed. Whatever the blackmailer might have taunted her with, when they were together, Tashi had given her heart to Akash. And had things gone on alright, she would have tried her best to marry him.

But with one confession, he had made every beautiful memory of the past feel like an illusion, as if everything she had held on to for so long was a mere facade, a palace built on lies.

Tashi had prided herself on being a good judge of people, but with Akash's confession, she couldn't help feeling disgusted at her choices of men.

She felt exhausted, all energy drained from her body. She lay on the bed, her head hitting the pillow with a soft flump, and wiped bitter tears from her eyes.

Her phone rang again. It was a WhatsApp call from a foreign number she hadn't seen before. Her breath caught in her throat - a gut feeling told her it was from the blackmailer. She was dazed after Akash's unsettling revelation and the prospect of attending a call from her tormentor filled with dread.

With shaking hands, she put the phone to her ear. "Hello?"

"Why haven't you replied to my emails?" the voice on the other end sounded muffled as if the caller had a cloth stuffed in front of his mouth. "Do you want me to come and ring your doorbell now, to show you I can do anything I want."

This was the first time she was speaking to her tormentor on the phone. She was horrified, her skin covered in goosebumps. "No, no. Please don't," she begged.

"Look out of your window."

Trembling with fear, she obliged.

"Do you see that black bike parked beside the curb? That's mine."

Her heart started beating frantically. "You- you are... Please don't... I will -" she sobbed. Fear - mind-numbing fear - the likes of which she hadn't experienced filled her veins like ice.

"You didn't buy what you needed, did you? I know your mother just left for the store. It will take at least half an hour for her to return. What if I stop by when dear little 'Tashu' is home alone?"

"No no no, please don't do that. I will do whatever you ask me to. Leave. Please leave," she sobbed.

"You better do whatever I tell you to. Otherwise, I'll be back. And next time, I'm not going to leave without you doing some nasty things for me like you did for Akash, do you understand?"

An unfeeling dial tone greeted her ears. She kept the phone away in haste, her chest heaving. She gulped as a figure dressed in blue jeans and a black jacket walked out from her building and climbed on the bike. A black helmet covered his face, obscuring his features. From the distance, he looked up and stared straight at her.

Tashi felt as if a chunk of ice was stuck in her spine, refusing to melt away, refusing to let warmth in.

Through the helmet, she could feel him sneering at her. Then, as if in slow motion, he started his bike, and, with a last glance her way, drove off into the distance.

Her fear was no longer a stranger on the internet. It had a face now; it was tangible, and it could physically harm her if it so intended.

She stood rooted to the window, staring at the dusty ground long after he had left.

Her phone pinged with a new message from the same foreign number. "Check outside your door," the message read.

Tashi was close to tears now. Her legs feeling like jelly, she walked up to the door and looked through the peephole. There was no one outside. Shuddering violently, she opened the door to find a neatly wrapped package placed at her doorstep. Looking around to make sure she was safe, she picked it up and stepped back inside, locking the door behind her.

She held her breath as she opened the wrapped package. It was a remote-controlled vibrator – a toy used by couples for sexual pleasure.

The thought of all the humiliating things her blackmailer could make her do with this filled her with dread.

Her heart felt like a heavy stone, slowly sinking to the bottom of a deep, black pond.

Chapter Six

The only way out of this mess

Sleep is an enemy these days,

it hardly stops by where I lay -

staring at the ceiling,

heart beating in rhythm to the relentless ticking of time-

as the hands of the clock gouge my face

like fingernails made of steel.

My thoughts flow out in black rivers:

some get lost in the darkness beneath my eyes,

and some come back to haunt me -

words stripped of meaning clogging my veins,

making my heart stop,

choking me up

as I try to take one desperate lungful of air

before I go down,

before I lose myself.

The sun has lost significance-

it comes up and goes down at will,

but my world remains dark all the same.

The bed, these sheets, my heart, this pain

are all I have,

and these words -

that shatter the silence into a billion shards,

with jagged edges I could slash my wrists with.

But escape is not an option

and release is not going to be easy.

I am going to go someday

but the world isn't kind enough

to let me leave my pain behind.

I have to fight it.

I have to live it.

And so I do.

Sleep is an enemy these days.

***

A week passed without the blackmailer contacting her.

Tashi spent her days in constant mental anguish, the vibrator wrapped up in its box stuffed inside her closet. It felt like a ticking time bomb – about to explode any instant at the whim of her tormentor. She kept waiting for his message, for another outrageous demand she knew was due.

Whenever she went to the office, every message on her phone made her jump in terror. Tashi hadn't gathered the nerve to approach the police for help. She was terrified that the blackmailer might somehow find out and do something drastic to get back at her. Ever since he had shown up at her doorstep, she no longer knew how close an eye he might be keeping on her, and in her current plight, she knew she was in no position to be reckless. A plan had to be worked out to get out of this situation, and Tashi was running out of ideas.

Akash's confession had turned her world upside down, making him feel more like a stranger than someone she had shared so much of her life with once upon a time. The shock and the constant paranoia were taking a toll on her work – with her team-lead asking on more than one occasion if she felt herself up to the challenges of the new project. Her competency was being put into question, and try as she might, getting back on track was proving to be difficult.

At home, her mother kept attempting to get her out of her foul mood, but she knew they were growing more and more distant with each passing day. They were each wrapped in blankets of their own anguish, trying hard to let the other in, but finding no way to do it. Though they lived in the same house, it was as if they were inhabiting two separate worlds.

The days were hard, the nights harder, and life had set itself into a cruel routine – one that felt suffocating and constrained, leaving her no room to breathe.

One night, Tashi came home to find her mother awake, busy in the kitchen preparing dinner. When she heard the door open, her mother wiped her hands on the apron and walked towards Tashi, a nervous smile on her face.

Tashi willed herself to smile back.

Without warning, her mother wrapped her arms Tashi's neck, pulling her into a tight embrace. Tashi stood for a while, her back stiff, hands hanging by her side, letting the warmth register, letting the love seep into the pores of her soul so clogged with shame and hate.

Then, she wrapped her arms around her mother's back and rested her chin on her shoulder.

Tashi hadn't wanted the hug, but she took it. She needed it.

After a moment, something unspoken seemed to pass between the them. Her mother pulled back and motioned for her to sit as she laid out a dinner for two.

Tashi didn't have the energy to plod through a conversation, so she asked, "Mom, why didn't you eat yet? It's late, and I was hoping to get some work done in my room over dinner."

"I know you are busy," her mother replied, "but I was hoping my daughter would have at least one meal with me after pretending like I don't exist for the past few weeks."

Her face betrayed no sadness, but with guilt, Tashi realised that the lines around her mouth had deepened, and her eyes had sunk in the black rings around them. She looked at least ten years older than what she remembered.

So caught up was she in her own troubles, that Tashi hadn't realised how hard the situation must have been for her mother. Last year, she had practically plucked her mother out from her life in Bomdila and convinced her to move to Delhi. "I promise I will keep you so entertained, you will not miss any of your friends," she had claimed with a wide smile. And true to her word, Tashi had taken care to introduce her to all the older ladies from the apartment complex, and take her out for a 'ladies' day out' every alternate weekend. But after the blackmailer had turned her world upside down, Tashi had barely spoken to her mother, let alone take her out on trips.

Gulping down remorse, she looked up and spoke, "Of course I have time, mom. I am terribly sorry about the past few weeks. I was so caught up in work that-"

Her mother put a wrinkled hand over her own and said, "I know you well, Ashi dear. You have always been smart enough to balance your work and life. But of late, you don't talk to me even when you are home, and all my attempts to start a conversation are rebuffed."

"Mom, I'm sorry I-"

"Please let me finish, dear," she interrupted her daughter with a raise of her hand. "I have known you since you were a baby. I can tell that something is very wrong now; you are hiding something from me."

Tashi stared, at a loss for words. "Mom, it's not like that, I-" she fumbled.

But her mother stopped her again. Her voice was kind and her eyes were filled with tears. "Whatever it is that is going on with your life, dear," she said quietly. "It is okay if you do not feel comfortable sharing. But I want you to know that I am here for you, no matter what."

Tashi suddenly found she could no longer speak, lest she burst into tears. Pouting slightly to mask her frown, she merely nodded and gripped her mother's hand tighter.

"Only for tonight," her mother continued, "will you forget the problem and eat with me like the old times?"

Tashi nodded once again, eyes swimming with tears she refused to shed.

"I know I have raised a strong girl, and I know you will emerge victorious from what is troubling you, dear," she said with a reassuring smile.

If only Tashi could share her mother's enthusiasm.

***

One Sunday afternoon, when Tashi was in her room taking an afternoon nap, her phone pinged with a message from an unknown number. She woke up with a start and sat on the bed, heart beating hard against her chest.

She was terrified, every fibre in her body screaming that it must be the blackmailer again. With trembling hands, she picked up the phone and unlocked the screen.

"Hey Tash. It's me, Manav. Guess what? I'm in Delhi for two weeks. Let's catch up tonight?"

For the first time in several weeks, Tashi heaved a sigh of relief after reading a text message on her phone.

Even after all the changes their jobs had brought into their lives, Manav had remained her best friend - the only person she could open up to with no qualms. But today, she felt weary - too exhausted to put on a mask, smile and pretend everything was all right when they met.

She wasn't ready to share her secret with him either.

So she took the easy way out. With a heavy heart, she replied, *"I'll be out for work the next few weeks. Sorry Manav, I can't make it."*

Lying to people who love you has become so simple, Tashi thought to herself for the second time that month. She was about to turn out the lights and go back to sleep when a sudden notification on her phone brought her back to her senses. She didn't even need to look at the screen to confirm.

It was an email from the blackmailer: *"Did you like the little present I left at your doorstep?"*

Tashi paused, horrified. The first line of the blackmailer's email left her throat dry. She gulped and read on.

"Tonight, I want you to do something special. I have seen how beautiful you look naked. I want that body of yours to dance according to what I

say. I have sent batteries with the present. You know what to do. Tonight, I want you to put on a show for my eyes only, bitch. I crave for you to scream and moan for me like you did in those videos."

Tashi turned away from the screen, her eyes burning with tears. This man was talking about her body as if it was his right to dehumanise her, to demean her, to make her hate her own self. She felt humiliated that someone had this much control over her life, and she didn't so much as know his name.

Her self–esteem was broken, reduced to nothing but damaged bits.

The mail went on: *"Do you want to know how much it would turn me on seeing you fuck yourself with a dildo on my command? I have attached an image with this email – so you can see how hot I find you."*

Heart filled with disgust, she looked at the picture he had sent. It was a photograph of his fist holding an old picture of herself. He had printed it out – and in it, she was wearing a night-dress, with one of her breasts popping out. Her right hand held the phone and her left was between her thighs.

Her face had a playful expression as if inviting the viewer to come and play with her.

And at the top corner of the image, covering her impish grin, she could see a load of viscous white liquid. With horror, she realised it was semen – as if the blackmailer had masturbated to her picture and orgasmed right on top of it.

Tashi's brain fogged up, and she could think straight no longer. Here was a faceless man who had so much access into her world; who was doing unspeakable things with her images. And the worst of it all was, he had enough power to ruin her life with just one click if he so wished.

Her chest felt uncomfortably tight.

Her head was spinning and she could feel her armpits were swathed in sweat. She hastily removed the cardigan she was wearing and walked to the kitchen sink, intending to splash some cold water on her face. But as soon as she let the tap run, her body trembled all over. She sat down on the floor, no longer trusting she could stand. Her heart was pounding hard against her rib cage. She tried closing her eyes to calm herself, but her breaths were sharp and shallow, her chest heaving with each laboured gasp. Her vision darkened, as if an invisible hand had turned out all light switches in the world. Bright stars popped in the darkness, swimming around in the blank space, making her head spin.

I'm dying, a voice in her head spoke. *This is what death feels like. This is how my mother will find my body. I am going to die alone.*

And then, slowly, Tashi sank to the floor, her hair flying in a messy bunch around her head. She could see nothing, hear nothing, save the unrelenting *tick-tock* of the clock by the refrigerator.

***

She didn't know whether it was an hour or ten before she came to her senses. Tashi felt disoriented, not sure whether it was day or night outside. The throbbing ache at the back of her skull was the only thing reminding her she was alive.

Pressing both her palms on the cold kitchen floor, she sat up weakly and attempted to steady herself. She dragged her frail body to the bed and somehow crawled underneath the sheets.

Her heart was beating wildly, but she gathered the strength to pick up her phone again. She had lost the will and courage to fight back, and all she could think of were ways to escape. With quivering fingers, she typed – *"Please let me go, I beg you. I will give you any amount of money you ask for. I will sell my apartment, I will take a fucking loan, but I will give you whatever you ask. Please leave me alone-,"* she broke down halfway, her helpless sobs filling the chilly air with despair. She didn't know how she managed to send over her half-typed email.

The blackmailer's reply came within a few seconds: *"If money was what I was after, I would have had other men fuck you already – many times over. Don't you get it, you slut? I don't want your fucking apartment, I want you. I want to be in control of your life; to be the only one who orders you around. I want to control every action of yours till you know you have no option but to obey me."*

A wave of nausea overcame her.

His message went on - *"Be prepared at seven in the evening. We are going to do a saucy video call."*

And from the deepest pits of her helplessness, Tashi managed to pull out the last ounce of courage. In a desperate attempt to hold on to what remained of her dignity, she typed, *"No. I refuse to do that. I am not getting on a video call with you. Please, just go away."*

With that, she kept her phone aside and took several deep breaths. She had a terrible feeling in her heart that if she pushed him too hard, there was no end to what extreme lengths the blackmailer could go to get what he wanted. And now, after he had turned up at her doorstep, she felt so anxious about what he might do next, that she almost considered sending him another mail and apologising.

But what would you do after that? A voice in her head asked. *Would you really strip for him and fuck yourself with a dildo when he is recording every second? He has already masturbated to a picture of your face; now he will do the same looking at you live and you are going to watch him. Do you want to let that happen?*

Tashi drew her knees close and hugged them so tight, her knuckles grew white as bone. "No," she screamed at the walls, breaking down in desperate sobs. "No, I will not let that happen."

The little yellow clock by her bedside table told her there were still five more hours before her mother would come back home from Sumi's wedding. She cried on, sitting curled up in bed in a position where the only thing that could give her some solace was the thought of escaping.

Escaping in any possible way, because all this fighting was only doing her more harm.

And then, as if intending to break her false sense of security, her phone rang. She turned to look at the screen - it was a call from a number she hadn't seen before. With an uneasy feeling in the pit of her stomach, she put it to her ear and mouthed in a trembling voice, "Hello?"

"Hi, is this miss Tashi?" a male voice asked. It sounded as if the speaker was young, possibly still in his early teens – his voice hadn't broken yet.

"Yes. Who's this?"

"Hi, I am from Gurgaon too. I am very interested in your... erm, proposal. Please tell me how and when we can meet?"

His words made no sense. Gaining her composure, she cut in, "Excuse me, what proposal are you talking about?"

"Uh, actually, I was talking about the one you put up online." He sounded uncomfortable as if talking to her required him to muster all his courage.

Her phone beeped with another call from a different number. "Hold on," she told the boy. "I am getting another call."

With that, she switched calls and answered, "Hello?"

"Tashi Chotten?" This time, it was a man who sounded a lot older and more confident. From the way he pronounced her name, she could tell he had had no previous interaction with anyone from Arunachal before.

"Yes, who's this?"

"I am interested in your offer, assuming you had uploaded the video yourself. I respect consent, and I don't think there's anything wrong if two adults mutually decide to hook up and have some fun. Plus, I always wanted to fuck one of your North Eastern chicks."

But Tashi had stopped listening to him after he had said the word 'video'. Her heart filled with horror, and she asked in a small, squeaky voice - "I'm sorry, but what exactly did you see? I haven't uploaded anything anywhere."

There was a silence on the other end, and within a few seconds, a dial tone greeted her ears. She let out a pained breath, her brain working furiously to digest what had just happened. Her phone beeped again – it was a message from the man who had called.

With a sense of dread weighing her shoulders down, she opened it. It contained a link to a website famous for its adult content.

A message from another new number had appeared on her screen before she could click on the link. She opened it, her heart already assuming the worst.

"Please send me your address and bank account details. I will arrive by 6 PM and would like to book you for three hours of service."

***

The wind was blowing wildly outside, knocking on her balcony door like an unwelcome intruder. Tashi felt herself gravitating towards it, till she opened the door and let herself out. The glare of the dying sun felt harsh on her face, and she lifted a hand to shield her eyes. All the birds had gone home, leaving the fiery sky devoid of music. And life.

To her right, several buildings were clustered together, making up the only neighbourhood she had known for the past two years. To her left, was the route she always took to her office. In front of her was the sky laden with crimson clouds and behind her was everything she wished she could run away from.

What if this was it?

What if this was all there is?

Tashi looked around. She was alone. She took her first step toward the edge of the balcony.

Her dark hair was flying wildly around her pale face. Her cheeks were tear-streaked, as if she had been crying for hours, but her eyes held determination. Strangely, they were dry.

Despite the sounds of heavy traffic below, the world was unnaturally quiet.

The icy wind licked her bare shoulders, making her shiver in the pre-winter chill. Her mother would have scolded her and asked her to wear a sweater lest she catch a cold. But somehow, the thought didn't bother her.

In fact, nothing bothered her except that she could take one step – just one – and this whole nightmare would be over in an instant.

She looked down at the bleak concrete below. She was ten floors above it, so close to ridding herself of the guilt and shame: it would save her reputation in front of the society and spare her mother from a lifetime of regret.

Tashi shivered as thoughts of her mother filled her head. She would be sad, yes, for there would be no closure. She would not understand why her daughter jumped to her death on a cold October evening.

Maybe she would blame her for being selfish, or maybe she would chide herself for not being selfless enough.

The chill got to her. She bit her lips and hugged herself tight. She remembered the warm hug her mother had given her yesterday when she left, and hot tears filled her eyes. *I wish I could hug mother one last time, she* thought.

The clock would strike seven any moment now. She was running out of time.

Heeding her persistent pleading, the blackmailer had deleted the video and her contact details from the website on one condition – that she should not back out from his request of a masturbation session over a video call. Anxious in her need to save herself at that moment, she had agreed.

But now that push came to shove, Tashi didn't know what to do.

She stood in the balcony for a few moments, letting the dusk wash over her. Another day died in front of her eyes, another meaningless 24 hours filled with hopelessness.

She leaned on the steel railing, feeling the cold metal pressing against her thighs through her sheer nightgown. It would be all over in an instant, she thought. Nothing mattered now except this moment, the dying sun, the cold wind on her bare shoulders and the fact that she, Tashi Chotten, had given up.

Her mother would arrive in another three hours. She was indeed running out of time.

Her body shaking violently with fear and resolve, Tashi took a step.

Chapter Seven

Tashi, you crazy woman

It was forty minutes past seven in the evening.

A woman stepped out of a twelve-storied building, her hair in disarray. A loose cardigan was thrown lazily over her shoulders as if she had put it on in haste. Her clothes were mismatched, and she had dark circles under her eyes.

Her gait was unsteady as if she were drunk. She walked with the air of one who had lost the will to live. Every few steps, she kept looking back as if to check if she were being followed. Then, looking ahead and gaining her composure, she walked on.

The woman's name was Tashi Chotten, and today, she had lived through one of the most gruelling experiences of her life. She had faced a storm head on and had come out victorious. It didn't matter that the victory was short-lived; that it rested precariously on the thin edge of a dagger.

What mattered was that after months of being made to feel small and defeated, Tashi had fought tooth and nail to carve out for herself a small victory.

On normal days, she would have booked a cab. But today, she had left her phone and all the nightmares it housed behind at home. She walked instead to the nearest metro station.

On normal days, she would have jumped at every noise, terrified of every peddler who tried to sell her something from their shop. But today, she was impervious to the noise. All she had ears for was the furious raging of the storm inside her head.

Today, she trundled on in a haze. Her her mind was clear, set on what she was out to achieve.

The metro station was a ten-minute walk from her home. To her frayed nerves, those ten minutes felt like an eternity, a lifetime wound into one long walk to a place she had been to so many times and, yet, felt like an unknown land hiding its demons.

The ride to her destination was uneventful. She found a place to sit in the women's compartment and stared ahead. No one paid her any heed, and she found some solace in being surrounded by other women too wrapped up in their own worlds to cast a suffering soul a second glance.

She reached where she had to get down after eleven stops. As she stepped out into the once-familiar streets again, a strong wave of nostalgia hit her. She had frequented these places in her college days, but it had been a while since she had found herself among the comforting aroma of incense mingled with fried *pakodas,* and that of cigarette smoke mixed with jasmine flowers.

Some young boys were playing cricket using wooden bats and makeshift stumps. She ducked as a ball threatened to fly close to her head, but it missed and landed next to her feet instead. She stopped in her tracks, picked it up and flung it back to the waiting boys. "Thank you, *Didi,*" one scrawny boy among them shouted and ran back to his group of waiting friends, who got engrossed in their game instantly.

Tashi took the first left and stopped in front of house number three. The walls were painted violet, the gate a warm shade of blue. The board hung outside said "Ahuja Residence".

She stepped inside and took a moment to take in all the familiar sights: the marigolds of late 2014 were replaced by flowering magnolias now. A row of flower pots with bright red roses nested cosily along the length of the front veranda.

Everything else looked the same as if the flowers in this house were the only things the passage of time had altered.

Tashi had been in front of these doors hundreds of times before, always greeted by a smiling Mrs Ahuja who ushered her in and treated her to a steaming cup of *masala chai*. Today, she didn't know who would welcome her in, or if there would be anybody to open the door at all. But this place was her only hope now, her last shot at ending the ordeal she was trapped in.

She held her breath and lifted a trembling hand to ring the doorbell.

For a moment, there was no answer. She turned around, faced the busy street and sat on the porch, prepared to wait till someone arrived. But in a few heartbeats, there were sounds of hustling from inside. She stepped up and faced the door as it opened in front of her.

A dark-haired, bearded and slightly plump man was standing in the doorway. He was dressed in a simple brown tee, black pyjama bottoms, and slippers. His left hand held his phone while his right was on the door, holding it open. He stared at her for a second before recognition flickered in his eyes. His face was lit up with surprise.

"Tashi," he exclaimed. Without waiting, he stepped forward and wrapped her in a hug.

Manav's affectionate embrace felt like home – like this was the comfort she had been seeking all these days. Tashi hugged him back, fighting tears of self-pity.

"Oh my gosh, I was so mad at you for not making time for me, but look at you now," he said, breaking off and smiling at her. "Come on in; my parents are out shopping now, but they will be here soon. Trust me, they will be delighted to see you."

She smiled weakly and followed him inside, looking around to gather her bearings. The house didn't seem to have changed much – the comfortable couches by the large windows, the polished mantle pieces smiling from the shelves on the walls, the royal blue Turkish carpet covering the floor – everything was in its place as Tashi remembered.

A million emotions were assailing her heart, but for the moment, she felt protected. Manav sat her down on the couch in front of the television set and handed her a cushion to cuddle, as had been his habit back in their college days. She accepted it and held it tight, feeling the need to squish it tighter than she would have usually done.

"Tashi, you crazy woman. How have you been? Why haven't you been answering my calls? I was angry before, but now I am thrilled to see you," he said, sitting down opposite her.

"Manav," she said in a weak voice.

"Is everything all right?" he asked, concern softening his gaze.

"No, Manav. Nothing is all right," she said, her hands covering her face. Her hair fell over her palms as she broke down into soft sobs.

He came to sit next to her, put his arm around her shivering form and let her weep onto his shoulder. When her sobs subsided, he told her in a soft voice, "Shh, Tashi. I am here now. You are safe."

***

Manav's parents had arrived some time back and after the customary hugs and greetings, he had dragged her into his room for want of some privacy. Two cups of hot chocolate and a half-finished plate of vegetable fritters lay on the table beside where they were seated.

Tashi had been talking for the better part of the past hour. "And today I had reluctantly got on a video call with him, not knowing what to expect. He had his camera turned off, of course. When I confronted him about the video he had uploaded, he told me it wasn't actually mine - just something he downloaded from another website and added my name and phone number onto it so other people would think I offer sexual favours for money. After that, I got so disturbed that I deleted every single account I had on social media, switched off my phone and came straight to your home. I want to run away, Manav. I cannot handle this any longer."

Stark shock was swimming in Manav's brown eyes. He had been listening intently to her all this while, stopping her at times to add questions of his own so he could understand her story better. She had been uncomfortable initially, but the concern and lack of judgement in his voice helped her open up.

"So, this guy was pushing you all along just so he could record a video showing your face?" Manav said, subconsciously scratching his chin. "Damn it, Tashi. This has gone on for far too long. We need to make it stop. Come with me, we are going to the police" he said, picking up his jacket and car keys.

"Now?" she asked, eyes wide with trepidation.

"Yes. Now," he replied, holding out a hand to help her out of her chair. "I want that bastard behind bars and I want it as soon as possible."

"But I am too afraid to tell my mother."

"You needn't be afraid, Tash. Whatever has happened until now – none of it is your fault."

"What if she is ashamed of me?" Tashi sobbed.

"No, Tashi. I have known Aunty for so long - she has always supported you no matter what. Don't you remember that time during our college elections when Tara and the other girls had blamed you for siding with the opponent lobby? The complaint was made to the Dean, but Aunty had stood her ground, refusing to believe you would do something like that till it was proved."

Tashi nodded weakly.

"I am sure," Manav continued, "that in these desperate times, she will stand by you with even more fierceness than before. She will be proud that you have been so brave."

"Will she?" Tashi gulped.

Manav gave her a small smile. "Sometimes, even though we feel like the entire world is against us, the battle isn't meant to be fought all alone. Strength can be found by opening our hearts to let the people who love us in."

"You make it sound so easy," she said, gratefully. Then, she bit her lip, suddenly unsure. "There is one more thing that has stopped me from going to the authorities for so long," she added.

Manav cocked his eyebrows, waiting.

"Supposing the police take action and put him behind bars; what is there to guarantee he wouldn't make my life hell once he is out?"

At this, Manav frowned and bent down to look her in the eye, "Tashi, I am also not sure about India's victim protection law. But the best way out now is to ask this to the people who might have some information."

She nodded. "Okay," she said, rising. "I am not sure if mom is home yet, though."

"We will wait if she hasn't arrived. And we will pick her up on the way to the police station."

"Manav," she whimpered. "I am afraid."

"Don't be. I told you before, didn't I? I am here, Tashi. You are safe."

***

Mrs Chotten's mouth was open in shock after Manav had finished narrating the story. Tashi was standing behind him, half hidden, staring at the ground with tears in her eyes.

"What are you talking about, son?" she asked, gesturing wildly with her hands. "Who did all these? Ashi, since when has this been going on?" She was almost shouting.

At this, Manav stepped forward and held her arms to calm her down. "Aunty," he whispered so her daughter wouldn't hear. "Tashi has been through a lot already. We have to stand by her and be strong, at least for her sake."

She stood there for a few moments, saying nothing, staring blankly from Manav to Tashi and back to Manav again. Then, comprehension dawned on her wrinkled face and her whole body started shivering. Her eyes filled with tears, she ran to Tashi and pulled her in an embrace.

"Oh, my daughter," she sobbed. "My poor, poor daughter."

***

Manav was driving with Tashi sitting beside. Mrs Chotten was at the backseat, silently wiping her tears. She was dressed in a pale pink *kurta* with matching leggings and a heavy travelling coat thrown over it. She had just arrived home and hadn't yet changed when Manav had rung the doorbell. "Ashi dear," she sobbed now, resting her hand on Tashi's right shoulder. "You handled so much stress all on your own. Why didn't you tell me before, baby?"

Tashi was crying too, but for the first time in several days, these weren't tears of shame or fear. She was crying because her mother had been with her all along; only she hadn't approached her for fear of how she might react.

Sitting in the car in the company of the two people who she loved the most in the world, Tashi felt like a human being after a long time, that she deserved something better than the constant humiliation and ridicule she was subjected to.

It was almost nine at night when Manav stopped his car in front of the police station. They got down and walked inside together, with Manav leading the way. Tashi followed, holding her mother by the arm. Several uniformed police officers were seated inside, and Tashi was nervous because she didn't know whom to approach for a complaint. Manav asked around and located a desk which they walked up to and filed an FIR with the officer-in-charge. They wanted to wait to talk to someone in a higher position, but the officer-in-charge asked them to leave.

"You may go home," they were told. "Someone will look into the case and get in touch with you."

But what if the blackmailer tries to contact her again? She cannot keep her phone switched off forever."

"Next time the blackmailer does something, inform us. We will have somebody look into it," the officer-in-charge informed them.

Chapter Eight

It is a dead end

Tashi was seated in the Delhi Police Cyber Crime Cell, wearing a simple green shirt with blue jeans, her hands folded neatly on her lap. Her mother, who had accompanied her to the police station, was waiting outside. Tashi sat across from Inspector Indrajit Bhowmick, with his scarred, yet polished desk separating them.

The inspector had a spacious office lined with shelves full of old folders and creased paperbacks in different colours. A golden framed logo was hung on the wall behind the inspector's chair with shiny letters proclaiming: *'Satyameva Jayate'* – 'Truth alone triumphs.' His window looked onto the street outside, with a tiny fraction of the iron sky visible from where she sat. Tashi glanced at an odd series of clouds. They looked like misshapen chimaeras breathing ashen fire onto the world.

Presently, he was leafing through a file of her case, with several lines he had jotted down during their past hour of interrogation. He twirled his moustache absent mindedly with his left hand and his otherwise clean-shaven face was set in a frown. His broad shoulders were pulled back, his posture perfectly upright. He squinted in concentration as they flew through the lines and lines of text, forming an opinion, drawing conclusions.

"Miss Tashi," the inspector said, looking up and holding her gaze. "These photographs the blackmailer sent you – were they clicked with a phone or camera?"

"They were clicked with a phone, officer."

"Whose phone was it?"

"Some of them were taken with my phone and some with my ex-boyfriend Akash's," she said, frowning, as she tried to remember. "But whenever we clicked a new picture, we used to share the images with each other. After we broke up, I deleted all the explicit images of us from my phone. I asked Akash to delete them too, but apparently, he didn't."

The inspector raised an eyebrow at this.

"Yes, sir," Tashi continued. "I had called him a few days back to ask about the blackmailing, and he said that he still had the photographs. In fact, he had shown some images to at least one of his friends."

"Okay," Inspector Indrajit said, noting the information down. He was trying his best to not make her uncomfortable. "Do you recall how many such images and videos were there?" he asked, lifting the pen to hold it between his pursed lips.

"We didn't have that many. But we were in a relationship for almost three years, so there must be around 250-300 – most of them were photographs."

"Before you deleted these images, was your phone ever stolen, or did you leave it unsupervised with somebody else?"

"No, sir, it was never stolen. I am a very private person, so I don't give my phone to anybody. It was always password-protected. And anyway, I used to delete the images regularly, so that there weren't too many photos at a time."

"Moving on," he said, "did you see the number on the blackmailer's bike when he drove off?"

"No sir," Tashi replied, biting her lower lip. "It was too far away for me to make out."

"You stated in your FIR that his bike was black. Did you see what make it was?"

"I am sorry, officer," Tashi replied, staring at her lap. "I can't recognise bike makes by looking at them."

"Hmm," Indrajit said, furrowing his brow. "One last question: is there anybody from your office or neighbourhood whom you suspect?"

Tashi thought for a moment before replying, carefully weighing her words "There are a few people in my office who pester me sometimes. But none of them know anything about Akash or my past to fish out those images."

"That will be all, Miss Tashi," the inspector said, scribbling something in his notebook. "You may leave now. But remember – you will inform me directly the next time the blackmailer contacts you, no matter how harmless his intention might seem. You have my number, right?"

"Thank you, sir. I do. And I will inform you as soon as he contacts me," Tashi said and got up to leave.

Raising his voice, the inspector called out to his subordinate, "Rajat. Take the contact details of the ex-boyfriend from Miss Tashi before she leaves. And call him as soon as possible to the station for some chit-chat."

Inspector Indrajit Bhowmick sat still in his chair long after Tashi left. He twirled his moustache subconsciously with his left hand, eyes staring out ahead, lost in thought.

***

"I haven't done anything, sir. Please believe me," he begged, sweat trickling down his face.

"Tashi said you had shared her images with your friends?" Inspector Indrajit Bhowmick replied. "See, Akash," he continued in a deathly calm voice. "If there is anything you are hiding from us, it will save you a lot of time and physical discomfort if you tell us right away. Otherwise, we have ways to extract information that will make you wish you had never been born."

"I shared none of her images with anyone, sir. I only showed it to one friend. I promise I did not even let him hold my phone while looking at the picture," Akash cried. He was trembling, his limp hair soaked in sweat and falling over his forehead. If Tashi saw him now, she would be amused to note it was straight today and not curly.

"Did you ever leave your phone unattended when that friend was around?" Inspector Indrajit asked. He was pacing around the room, his arms crossed, the fingers of his right hand tapping impatiently on his elbow.

Realisation dawned on Akash's face as he mouthed, "Yes sir, I might have."

Indrajit walked up to the table and sat opposite Akash. "Did he know the password to unlock your phone?"

"Yes sir," he said in a small voice, eyes filled with shame. When the inspector said nothing, as if waiting for more information, Akash continued, "I might have shared it with him on a couple of occasions when he had to use my phone."

Indrajit looked him in the eye. Then, without warning, he brought his fist down and slammed the table hard. Akash jumped in his chair, his whole body trembling with fear. "Please believe me," he sobbed. "If I knew something like this would happen, I would have never stored those images in my phone."

Indrajit looked at him for a full minute. Then he got up slowly and adjusted his shirt. With his right hand, he picked up his Police cap from the table separating them and left the room, leaving a whimpering Akash staring behind him.

"The suspect appears too soft-skinned to lie to the police, sir. Do you believe him?" sub-Inspector Rajat of Delhi Police Cyber Crime Cell asked.

"In cases of revenge porn, the ex-lover is usually the culprit trying to get back at the women who rejected them," Indrajit said. "But this couple broke up almost four years back. And this man is speaking the truth – I can see it in his eyes. The possible suspect now is the friend, Ravikant. Make sure you do a background check on him and pay him a visit."

"I will, sir," Rajat said.

"My instinct tells me this is a different case altogether, Rajat," he said frowning. "Did you check the CCTV footage in front of the victim's house on the day the blackmailer turned up at her doorstep?"

"I did, sir," Rajat said, eyes downcast. "But there are no cameras in the area covering that particular view of the road."

"Okay. Has the report on those phone numbers the blackmailer used come back?"

"Yes sir," Rajat replied opening the file in his hand and flipping through the first few pages. "Most of the messages that were sent to the victim's phone were from untraceable international numbers. But on the day when he came around her house, he had called her using an Indian number. The person in whose name this sim card is registered was reported dead two years back."

"Hmm," Indrajit said, looking through the report. "So, he used this dummy sim card only once and discarded it?"

"No sir, he used this number five times," Rajat said pointing at a circled number on the file with his index finger. "The sim was activated once in Patel Nagar and another time at Cyber City. But on the rest of the three times, it got activated at Sector 29, Gurgaon. Twice, he used it to send a message to the victim after 11 at night. So, I am guessing that might be where his home is located."

Indrajit nodded, his eyes crinkled in thought. "Sector 29 is a large area. We can't go knocking on every door to see if we have our criminal. Do we have any leads on the emails he sent?"

"All of them were sent through an anonymous email system. I called them this afternoon to ask which IP address was used to send emails at those particular times. But when we tracked the IP address, we reached Tor's exit node."

"Hmm," Indrajit said. "That happens because the Tor proxy bounces all traffic through the Tor network and then out into the network, making it virtually impossible to know what information is being accessed and who accessed it."

"Exactly, sir. The blackmailer was brilliant. There is no way to track the IP address through which he sent his emails. Every lead we had hit a dead end," Rajat replied in a dejected voice.

"I hadn't expected him to be this careful," Indrajit said, thinking hard. "Majority of the cases of cybercrime against women go unaccounted for because the victim is too terrified to register a complaint. We cannot have it easy, Rajat. We have to catch the criminal and teach him a lesson."

Sub-Inspector Rajat opened the folder in his hands with a dejected look on his face. "I agree, sir," he said. "But there is no way to know which Tor user is accessing what website."

Indrajit paced on for a while and then stopped in his tracks. He turned to face Rajat, eyes lit with excitement. "What if we turn his weapon into his weakness?" he said.

"I didn't quite get you, sir," Rajat replied, looking up from the files.

"What I mean to say is, the criminal tried very hard to maintain anonymity," Indrajit said with a faint smile, stretching his muscular arms. "But what if we use his anonymity to find his identity? The list of Tor entry and exit nodes is public, isn't it?"

"Yes sir."

"That means the internet service providers can't tell us which websites have been accessed, but we can find out which users in Sector 29 have been using Tor on those dates, right?"

Rajat quipped in, "Right. And only a few internet users are aware how to use Tor. Then that would mean-"

"Our list of suspects would be narrowed down by as much as 90%," Indrajit finished the sentence for him with a faint smile.

Rajat wiped the perspiration on his forehead with the back of his sleeve as Indrajit paced the room again, talking very fast. "I want you to contact every internet service provider covering Sector 29 and find out which users have routed their traffic through Tor in the past month. Use all your Cyber Cell clout, Rajat, but get me this information by tomorrow."

Rajat saluted as Indrajit left the room, his eyes glinting with the adrenaline rush.

***

In an act of defiance, Tashi had turned her phone back on that night after returning from the police station. There were no new messages or calls from the blackmailer.

It was surprising how much strength her mother's support seemed to lend to her frayed nerves. That night, the two of them had dinner together after a long time. In haste, her mother prepared a simple meal of rice and steamed vegetables, but to Tashi, that tasted better than anything she had eaten in months. She didn't sleep in her own room that night, for the fear of unknown demons still assailed her. She and her mother shared a blanket, and for the first time since the blackmailer had contacted her, Tashi had a peaceful, dreamless sleep.

She went to work the next day. It was difficult to mask her anxiety every time her phone vibrated, but she held herself together. Inspector Indrajit had called her up in the morning informing her of the leads they were working on. "We expect to have the criminal behind bars within this week," he had asserted. His confident tone had given her some hope.

Manav had been in touch throughout the day, asking her for updates and telling her to be strong. Tashi had isolated herself from human contact for so long, that this sudden rush of concern felt overwhelming. When he asked if they could meet in the evening, she had almost refused, saying she was busy. But she held herself back at the last moment. *I cannot live my entire life crawling inside a shell,* she thought as she agreed to meet Manav at a cafe later that day.

That evening, for the first time since the blackmailer had contacted her, Tashi spent some time in front of the mirror admiring her reflection before heading out. She had showered after office and put on a knee-length black dress that hugged her slender curves. She painted her lips a dark shade of red and pouted in front of the mirror, striking a pose, sucking her tummy in. Satisfied, she put on her black heels and stepped out in the warm Gurgaon air.

Manav was waiting in the street below, dressed in black jeans and a casual brown shirt with white checks. He was fiddling with his phone, but when he saw her, his eyes lit up. Tashi greeted him with a hug and surprised him by smiling.

Once they were both settled in and Manav had gunned the engine to life, he looked towards her and asked, "How are you holding up?"

"I'm doing good," she replied nervously, "I suppose."

"Well you certainly look a lot better than you did yesterday." She smiled faintly at this. "Did you get any more messages since we last talked?"

She shook her head. "Well, let's not ruin this evening by talking of things that aren't in our control," Manav said as he placed his hand over hers and gave it a slight squeeze.

Tashi smiled and replied, "Yes, please." With her left hand, she adjusted her hair and looked towards him. "I was so caught up in my troubles yesterday, I didn't even ask anything about you. Tell me, how's everything?"

The rest of the car ride passed by in a blur as Manav updated her on the goings on in his office and life in general.

When they reached the café, a waiter smiled perfunctorily at them and held the door open as Manav held two fingers up and mouthed, "Table for two."

Tashi walked in confidently, but the lights, the music and the constant murmur of the people huddled inside made her uneasy. She shivered as Manav led the way to their table, and sat down, feeling the old anxiety return. She knew everyone else was engrossed in their own world, but, to her, it felt as if they were sneaking sideward glances at her, as if they knew her secret and were smirking amongst themselves at her plight. The more she tried to hide it, the more constricted her chest felt. She held on to her facade of being brave, till at one point, she burst into tears in the middle of a story Manav was narrating. He stopped and extended his hand across the table to take her hand in his. He held it until she was done crying and said, "I can only imagine the pain you must be going through. But, have faith, Tash, things will be all right soon."

"What if this is the calm before the storm? What if he gets angry and does some irreparable damage?" she asked him.

"Then we will take him down. I called Inspector Indrajit this morning to ask about the progress they were making. He assured me they had things in control and even if the blackmailer did something rash like uploading your pictures online, the Police will get them removed as soon as possible with a legal notice."

Tashi thought about the damage the pictures could do to her reputation in a few hours. She closed her eyes and shook off the terrifying thought. "Just trust me on this, Tash," Manav was saying. "We will let nothing bad happen to you."

Though her eyes still held a worried look, she wiped her tears and gave his hand a little squeeze. "I am so grateful I have you."

"As you always will," he assured her.

"I feel so scared," she said in a small voice, eyes downcast, lips set in a frown.

"I would be lying if I said I am confident. But we have the authorities on our side. And more importantly, you have your mother's support. You'd be surprised if you knew how much easier life gets when we have our loved ones ready to be the parachute when life throws us hurtling down the abyss."

She looked up with a small smile and nodded, not trusting herself to speak lest she burst into tears again.

Manav gave her a reassuring smile. "If you don't let me finish this story now, I promise I will call you at night and keep talking until it is finally done. Don't blame me for your dark circles the next morning."

This time, Tashi had to struggle not to laugh at the irony.

***

When Inspector Indrajit entered his office the next morning, his subordinate, Rajat, was already present with a report. His bushy moustache was combed to perfection, and he had a faint smile on his face when he saluted. "Sir, I called the friend of the ex-boyfriend who had seen the pictures to the station and grilled him for five hours. I am pretty sure he isn't aware of this. Also, I had the location records from his phone checked. The man was in his home on the day the blackmailer appeared in front of the victim's house."

The inspector frowned. "Why do you look so happy then?" he demanded.

"I had to resort to some underhand tactics, sir, but I found out which people in Sector 29 used Tor on those particular dates in the last month."

"How many people are we talking about?"

"Only two, sir," Rajat replied with a triumphant smile. He handed him the report file and pointed to the information that had been highlighted. "One of them is a college student, He has been staying in Gurgaon in a one-room apartment for the past 5 weeks. And the other works in some IT company and has been living in his 1-BHK apartment since the last three years."

"Hmm," said Indrajit, thinking hard. "Did you check if either of them has a black motorbike?"

"I did, sir," Rajat replied. "Neither of them do. It must have been rented or borrowed."

"Hmm," Indrajit said. "The college kid has been here for 5 weeks, you say? When was the first time the victim got the threatening email?"

"Around 5 weeks back, sir," Rajat replied.

"Looks like we have found our man," Indrajit said. "Let's not waste any more time. The victim has been through enough trauma already. I will get us search warrants and we will pay both the suspects a 'surprise visit' as soon as possible."

When Rajat left the room, Indrajit was already calling the authorities up for permissions.

Chapter Nine

Just some drunk men

Karan Mondal was a final year engineering undergraduate from Durgapur doing his internship at a company in Gurgaon. He had rented an apartment for two months in Sector 29. As was his habit, he sat down on his computer for his usual evening schedule while sipping coffee from a large mug. His room was dimly lit with wires strewn all over the floor. His laptop cover had at least ten different stickers of famous electronics brands. His place smelled of cigarettes. There were several crumpled packets of previous food delivery orders thrown carelessly around the floor.

Karan slouched shirtless in his chair and opened an incognito window on his browser. He entered his search item when there were a series of sharp raps on his door.

Startled, Karan sat up.

He had no friends in the city and the only person who ever knocked on his door was his maid who came to clean up in the weekends. Today, the knocks were incessant, and he could hear a rough male voice from outside saying, "Open up."

Not sure of what to expect, Karan picked up a shirt from the messy dump of clothes on his bed and opened the door. To his shock, there were two Police officers standing outside. Without warning, the taller of the two grabbed his collar and shouted in his face, "You are Karan, aren't you? We know what you have been up to since the past five weeks. Rajat, confiscate his computer and every electronic gadget you find. And you, Mr Karan, you are coming with us."

***

29-year-old Amish Grover walked inside his apartment and turned on the lights. He kept his car keys and wallet on a small table by the door. He sat on the couch in his living room and massaged the back of his neck. With a new merger coming up, the last few days had been hectic at the office. Today, he had had long meetings with some clients that had taken up all evening. With a sigh, he took out his phone and was about to place an order for dinner when his doorbell rang.

Amish wasn't expecting any guests. He stood up wearily and stretched his hands. Then, he walked to the door and looked through the peephole. An irrational fear gripped his chest when he saw two uniformed police officers standing outside. One of them was tall and muscular, a neatly trimmed moustache sitting on his otherwise clean-shaven face. The shorter one had a bushy moustache and the air of polished obeisance about him. The muscled officer rang the doorbell once more and Amish opened the door.

"Inspector Indrajit Bhowmick of Delhi Police Cyber Crime Cell," the officer said flashing an ID. "We have a search warrant for you, Mr Grover. It's a routine investigation, but you must come with us. Rajat, check all the electronics and bring them to the station."

***

"Are you going to confess, you piece of shit?"

"Yes sir, I confess. I confess," Karan, the college student, sobbed. The top two buttons of his shirt had flung open, revealing matted chest hair drenched in sweat. "Please don't hit me, sir, I am sorry."

"It's people like you who make me lose faith in humanity," Indrajit spat. He grabbed Karan by the collar and pulled his face closer. "Tell me, how many other women have you done it with?"

There was a look of confusion on his childish features. "How many other – sir, what do you mean?"

"How many other women have you blackmailed, tell me? I have neither the mood nor the patience to deal with your pathetic pretences," the inspector spat.

"Sir, I am not pretending. I honestly have no clue what you are talking about. I have never blackmailed any man or woman in my life," he cried.

Indrajit straightened, loosening his grip on Karan's collar. "What did you confess to just now, then?"

"F-For illegally downloading porn using torrents?" Karan replied, his face a mask of shame and confusion.

"Do you know who Tashi Chotten is?" Indrajit asked, his tone flat.

"Tashi what? This is the first time in my life I heard that weird name. I swear on my mother, sir."

***

"But he had confessed to being guilty, hadn't he, sir?" Rajat asked.

"Apparently, the kid thought we arrested him for illegally downloading porn using Tor," Indrajit said, frowning.

The two of them were standing outside the interrogation room. A shivering, weeping Karan was seated inside, the glass of water on his table untouched.

"We must interrogate the next suspect. He works in a reputed IT firm, sir."

"I know. Something doesn't fit here, Rajat. Amish Grover's record is too clean to be true. You said you had our experts check through his computer and phone?"

"Yes, sir. They combed through all his hard drives but found nothing. According to the ISPs, he had been using Tor, but he claims it was only to download some movies. He denies having ever seen Tashi."

"Hmm," Indrajit said, rubbing his forehead with his thumb. "Did his house have a printer?"

"Yes, sir, it did."

"And what about Karan's?"

"The kid only had a laptop and some external hard drives, sir; no other gadgets."

"Okay. Go to Grover's house with a team and search through everything he owns, even the trash. We might be missing something important here."

"Yes sir," Rajat saluted and left as Indrajit picked his phone to make a call.

***

Tashi stood before the man the Police suspected was the blackmailer. He hadn't confessed yet and there wasn't sufficient proof either. "Do you recognise him?" the inspector asked.

A wave of emotions overwhelmed her: was this it: the moment when the truth would unfold and her ordeal would end? Her heart beat faster with anticipation.

The suspect was slouched in a chair inside the interrogation room, staring into blankness, unaware he was being watched. He must be in his late 20s with a svelte beard and a crisp shirt that was ruffled now – proof that he had remained overnight in police custody. There was no telltale sign on his face that he might be the one who had caused her so much pain. *In fact,* Tashi thought, *if I had seen him in some other context,*

I might have even found him attractive. What need did a man like that have to resort to blackmail?

Tashi shook her head.

***

The suspect, Amish Grover was seated inside the interrogation room and Indrajit was leafing through some reports outside when Rajat returned. "Sir," he saluted, "we found some interesting items in the suspect's home."

Indrajit turned to look at the evidence Rajat and his team had gathered.

Then, his weathered face broke into a cold smile. He entered the interrogation room. Amish's face registered fear as Indrajit loomed closer and said in a voice that sent chills down his spine, "You claim that you don't have anything to say, eh? Well, don't worry. We have some fascinating ways of bringing your memory back."

***

"You deny having anything to do with the blackmailing, eh?" Indrajit shouted.

Amish was clutching his throbbing cheek, sweating profusely under the light of the single bulb pointed at his face. A thin stream of blood trickled down his chin, losing its way in the tangle of his beard. Even then, he held his resolve. "I don't know what blackmail you are talking about."

"How do you explain this then?" Indrajit said, pulling out a Ziploc bag with a crumpled sheet of paper. It was a printed photograph showing Tashi in with half her clothes off.

Amish gaped, words suddenly failing him. "What – what is this? This doesn't prove anything," he said at last.

"It proves everything, Mr Grover. The victim had stated in her FIR that the blackmailer had jerked off on a photograph of hers and sent a picture to show it. How do you explain that picture appearing in the trash-can in your bedroom?"

Amish's resolve was crumbling. He stared at his feet, mind working furiously to think of an excuse.

Slap.

Indrajit's hand landed sharply on his cheek. His head fell back, and an inadvertent grunt of pain escaped his parted lips. The pain was so intense, his eyes started watering. He had bitten his tongue hard in the impact. A new trickle of blood joined the stream that had turned brown under the piercing light.

"We are having a forensic team look at the DNA on the semen on this photograph and match that with yours. Do you want to wait until then or will you save us both time and effort and confess?"

"I – I – I want to call my lawyer," Amish stuttered.
Indrajit slapped him again, harder this time. Amish's form slumped lower in his chair, eyes tearing up with pain.

"Do you think this is a bloody Bollywood movie where you get a chance to call your lawyer?" Indrajit demanded, leaning close and clutching his collar. "You have two choices: either tell me everything or I will beat it out of you, you filthy scum." He raised his fist in the air.

Amish ducked, anticipating the blow. "Please, sir, stop. I will tell you everything," he said, tears running down his cheeks. When he looked up, there was resignation in his eyes. Strangely though, there was no remorse. He had the look of a man knowing his game was up and yet having no second thoughts about having made a wrong move. "But first, let me ask you this: what gave me away? How did you narrow it down in the first place?"

Slap.

Indrajit's blow landed so hard on Amish's face, that his head was flung back, sweat beads flying in the air. The inspector turned his chair around and sat to face the criminal. "Do you honestly think you are in a position to ask me questions?" he asked.

With a trembling voice, Amish Grover shrugged and started narrating his story.

***

This started around five months back when I was at a colleague's party at a bar in Gurgaon. Everyone had had quite a few drinks, and I was roaming around aimlessly when I came across a small group of four black-suited men laughing the loudest. I joined them and one guy introduced me to everyone. All of them were discussing women – just some drunk men trying to make their sex lives sound cooler than they are. The one called Ravi was telling a story about a woman he met on a solo trip to Kasol, and everyone else was egging him on for juicier details. After his story was done, it was another man's turn to share his anecdote. This one was called Akash.

"Tell us about that hot chick in your office," Ravi said, downing his sixth whiskey of the night.

"I had scored her a few nights back. Man, what curves that one has," Akash said, pulling out his phone and showing a selfie of him with an attractive woman. "Isn't she hot?" he asked. The others looked at the image and remarked, "Fuck man, her assets look smoking hot in that revealing top. Pretty sure you had lots of fun playing with them"

Akash blushed.

"Bro, you have become a big player these days!" Ravi remarked, slapping him on the back.

After a general round of laughter that followed, the other two men excused themselves from our little gathering, saying they had a long journey ahead as their home was in South Delhi. Only the three of us remained – Ravi, Akash and I.

The music in the club changed, and the DJ started playing a dance number. Several young people dashed onto the dance floor, among them, the most eye-catching was a group of girls from the North East.

"Damn, these North Eastern girls are hot," Akash remarked.

"But whatever you say, she was something else, man," Ravi nudged Akash with his elbow and winked, his hands tracing a big hourglass shape in the air.

Akash's face lit up when he talked about her. "Oh damn, that chick, man, that was one hot ass."

Curious, I asked, "Who is this chick?"

"There was this one girl from the North East. Bro, she had such plump thighs. This lucky bastard fucked her for three years," Ravi slurred happily.

"Oh really?" I asked. "Show us some pictures then."

At this, Akash laughed and pulled out his phone. In his drunk state, he found it difficult to scroll through all the images in his gallery, but he finally settled on one and showed it to me. It was an image of a younger version of him with his arm around the waist of a beautiful woman. "She is really something," I said.

The woman in question was breath-taking, and I was intrigued enough to want to look at more pictures. To challenge Akash's male ego into obliging my wish, I taunted him, "Bro, no offence, but there is no way such a stunner would date a guy like you."

Ravi burst into laughter at this, spluttering some drink into the air. He wiped his mouth with the back of his hand and eyed Akash, who looked indignant. He took his phone and told us - "I am going to call her right now and prove it to you that she and I used to date."

After that, he must have called her up at least twenty times, but there was no answer. Akash looked dismayed. To goad him further, I shook my head and arranged my face into a sympathetic smile. I patted him gently on the back. "There's nothing to be embarrassed about, bro," I said in the most patronising tone I could manage. "I am sure even the best of us sometimes pretend to have banged a chick so clearly out of our leagues."

Akash looked indignant, enraged at the audacity of my claim. To calm him down, Ravi said, "Chill, bro. Show us those pictures you clicked on that beach holiday," he said and scrolled through Akash's gallery with cigarette-stained fingers. I leaned in for a closer look and what I saw took me by surprise: there were nudes in that folder.

Ravi and Akash showed more pictures of him holding that beautiful, scantily clad woman. But I couldn't get an image I had just seen out of my mind: of a curvy woman being fucked from the behind with her hair held in a man's fist. Akash was so drunk, that when was clicking on another image to show us, his phone slipped through his fingers and fell to the floor. He was slouched on a beanbag, so I offered to pick it up. As I bent to retrieve the phone, the folder from which he had selected the photo was open on the screen. I looked at it for a second longer. He had over 300 images and videos of this beautiful woman in several erotic positions. I got aroused at the thought of seeing so many pictures of a naked woman and decided that I had to see more.

I gave his phone back and waited till the party cleared up. The bar was almost empty when I asked them where they lived. Ravi said he was from Sushant Lok and Akash had his house in Sohna Road. Although my place was in Sector 29, I lied that I lived in Sohna Road too and offered to share a cab with Akash.

"Dude, you book the cab. I don't know where I will take us to if I am left unsupervised tonight," he laughed.

Jumping at the chance, I said, "Bro, my battery has run out. Can I use your phone?"

"Sure," he said and handed over his phone. I noted that it had a fingerprint lock. I booked a cab and dragged an almost unconscious Akash to the car when the driver arrived. He sat down and started talking some gibberish, when I said in a soft voice, "Bro, you have drunk a lot. You should sleep – our destination is at least an hour away."

His phone was still in my hand when he passed out. I waited a few minutes before I could hear him snoring softly. Then, I lifted his hand to press his forefinger on the fingerprint panel to unlock his phone. It was a tempting thought to enjoy the pictures right then, but I held back. I set up a Bluetooth transfer of the first fifty pictures and videos to my phone. The transfer was completed in around forty minutes, and once I was done, I deleted the transfer history and put the phone back in Akash's front pocket without waking him up.

I knew he wouldn't remember any of this the next day.

"That is how I came to have Tashi's pictures," Amish told Inspector Indrajit Bhowmick in a low voice.

The confession enraged the inspector. He was tempted to strike again, to inflict more damage on this sick bastard. He grit his teeth to hold himself back, mentally repeating something he had learned in training - that unjustified violence wasn't mandated by the law. "That is when you decided to take the life of an innocent woman in your own hands? What did you wish to achieve, huh, you psychopath?" he spat.

"Nothing, actually," Amish mouthed, refusing to meet the inspector's eye. "I enjoyed those photographs and videos for many months until I had got bored with them. I wanted more, and the idea of getting explicit content directly from that North Eastern woman was more intriguing than watching porn. The one thing that took me longer was that I wasn't sure what her full name was. I remembered it was Tashi-something, but her last name somehow eluded me. And then, suddenly, it came back to me - Chotten, Tashi Chotten."

"Did you snitch her contact details from Akash's phone as well?" Indrajit demanded.

"No, I had no intention of blackmailing her then. But the name, Tashi Chotten, was so unique, that all I had to do was simply search it on Facebook. Her profile wasn't private, and I got her phone number and email ID with one click."

"What about her house address?"

"That was simple. She had shared some of her Instagram photos on Facebook where she had geo-tagged the location of her house. It was only a matter of days before I went to her building and spent a few hours strolling in front of it – to know her timings and which floor she lived in. The thrill of seeing the woman I had fantasised about so often in real life was something else, I tell you, inspector. She was even more good-looking now that she was older, and I knew I craved badly for her."

"And just like that, you decided to blackmail Tashi for five long weeks?"

"Not blackmail, inspector," Amish said looking up to meet the inspector's eyes. The lines around his mouth appeared to be etched with a cold confidence. "I decided that she has had enough fun, and now it was my turn to have some fun with her," he said. A distinctly cruel note had crept into Amish's voice that made the inspector sit up. "Anyway, women like Tashi who sleep around with men they have no intention of marrying need to be taught a lesson. They go around breaking hearts like it's second nature to them. Such women deserve to be given a taste of their own medicine, Inspector, don't you think?"

Indrajit winced. "So, you perverted fuck took it upon yourself as your job," he cussed.

"Who else would do it if not me?" Amish said in an unwavering voice.

Just then, the door opened and Rajat entered the room carrying a file. He called Indrajit to the corner and whispered in his ear, "Sir, the criminal was careful in erasing all evidence from his laptop, but our team recovered an external hard drive hidden behind a painting in his bedroom," he said, handing him the file. "The data was encrypted, but this fool had used the same password as his social media accounts. Our experts found photographs and screenshots of email drafts proving that this man has been blackmailing not only Tashi but three other women. This has been going on for the past three years, probably even longer. And also, sir, there are photographs of unsuspecting women changing clothes or taking showers captured from open windows. I believe he either blackmailed those women or simply went on clicking more pictures without their permission."

Indrajit stared at the evidence in his hands, aghast. Shaking his head, he said slowly, "Make sure you assign teams to investigate the other cases. I want no stone to be left unturned in this regard."

He took the file from Rajat and slammed it on the table in front of Amish, making dust fly in a small cloud around his face. The man looked up and stared Indrajit in the eye. All traces of the shaking, sweaty Amish of a few minutes ago was gone, and Indrajit was left staring into the eyes of a cold-hearted criminal.

"You turned out to be a serial blackmailer," Indrajit shouted.

"Blackmailer doesn't sound classy, inspector. I am a man who likes to have his fun. And for me, the high of having a helpless woman under my control is the most addictive – when she doesn't love me, and yet, is ready to do anything I ask her to. It gives me a kick like nothing else," he said with a twisted half-smile.

"And let's face it, inspector, I am sure Tashi Chotten must have enjoyed being the centre of attention of a man for so long."

He had made her name sound like a curse.
"You creep," Indrajit growled. "You are charged under Section 66 A for deliberately sending emails to cause annoyance to a person, section 67 A for circulation of obscene content, section 509 for insult to the modesty of a woman, section 500 for attempts at defamation, and section 67 B for attempting to distribute obscene content."

Amish looked up with defiance in his eyes. "I will be locked up for five years at the most. But will you be able to give those five weeks back to Tashi?"

"You are going to be locked up for many, many years, you vermin. And I will make sure I use every ounce of influence I have to make sure your term is non bailable."

The criminal slumped back in his chair with a strange light in his eyes that Indrajit couldn't quite place – was it guilt?

Why did it look so much like pride then?

Chapter Ten

Blackcurrant or chocolate?

Tashi and Manav were seated opposite Inspector Indrajit in his office. He sat facing them from across the polished desk, his uniform crisp.

The police had called Tashi in the morning to inform that the blackmailer had been found and put behind bars. After hanging up, she had immediately called Manav and asked him to accompany her to the police station.

"The blackmailer worked in the sales department of a reputed IT company," Indrajit said, showing them the first page of criminal's file. "He had a well-paying job, and his friends would have been prepared to swear that they knew the man well. On the surface, he was an average IT professional with a normal day-to-day life and nothing to hide."

Manav nodded, while Tashi looked at the inspector with rapt attention, her shaking hands hanging by her side.

"But inherently," the inspector continued, "he was a hardened criminal – a pervert who derived pleasure by preying on unsuspecting women and blackmailing them into doing his bidding."

Tashi stifled a sob. Manav put a protective arm around her and gave her shoulder a little squeeze.

"This man was an animal hiding in plain sight," Manav said. "It is heartbreaking to imagine how many more lives he might have ruined had Tashi not gathered enough courage to bring this matter to the police."

"Exactly," the inspector said. "In most cases like these, the victims are afraid their identities might be publicly disclosed or their reputations might suffer if they reported the case to the police. They aren't aware that their silence is doing them more harm than raising their voices would ever do."

Tashi nodded vigorously, her fists balled tight, the skin stretched over her knuckles.

"The sad thing is that the criminal got only the first batch of photos from Akash's phone," Indrajit said, looking Tashi straight in the eye. "The rest of the information – like your phone number and address – was handed to him on a platter by your social media handles."

Tashi nodded, head hung in shame. "I had never thought keeping my Instagram profile public would have such repercussions," she said.

The Inspector looked thoughtful when he said, "This generation of young women fail to realize how important it is to keep their personal details private. The fact that Akash didn't delete those old photographs was his fault, but the fact that you left your phone number and address so easily discoverable by the world is..." he trailed off, but his meaning was apparent.

Tashi looked ready to burst into tears. To ease the tension in the air, Manav cleared his throat and said, "Inspector, what options do you think are open to a woman who finds herself the victim of cyber-attacks like Tashi did?"

"Today, there are helpline numbers solely designed for women to anonymously lodge complaints. In fact, there are websites where friends or family can lodge a report if they suspect some crime like this is being committed."

"I wish the society viewed such crimes differently too," Manav added. "Rather than shaming the woman for having her pictures splashed all over revenge porn websites, people should extend their support and shame the criminal instead. If this simple action takes away the sense of power the perverts feel from having a woman under their control, it might lead to lesser instances of such cases repeating."

Inspector Indrajit nodded and shook hands with both of them. Tashi gave him a weak smile and asked, "There is one last question I had, officer," she said.

Inspector Indrajit nodded, urging her to go on.

"What is there to guarantee that this man would not do something even more horrific to get back at me if he is released on bail?"

At this, the inspector frowned. "The prosecution will actively attempt to oppose the bail of the criminal," he said at length. "And even if, by some miracle, he succeeds in getting bail, he has to sign a bond that forbids him from continuing the offence or harming the witness in any way. If he violates these conditions and contacts you in any form, please inform me immediately. I will see to it that the court forfeits his bail amount, cancels his bail and adds to his crime count. If he does something so foolhardy, he will be thoroughly screwed on the day of judgement."

Tashi looked at Manav. He gave her a small, almost imperceptible nod. "We thank you for your help, inspector," he said, rising.

"The police department salutes the strength of will you displayed throughout this case," Indrajit said, standing up. "You may rest assured that this man would not trouble you again," he bade them goodbye with a smile.

When they stepped out of the police station, the sun was still shining weakly through the clouds, but to Tashi, the day seemed to have grown infinitely brighter.

She looked at Manav, tossed her black hair hair out of her face and smiled, "Why don't we grab some ice cream on the way back home."

He grinned at her, "Blackcurrant or chocolate?"

"Like the old times, chocolate."

Epilogue: And After

It was a chilly Friday afternoon, almost eight months after the blackmailer had been caught. In their cosy two-bedroom apartment, Mrs Chotten was shelling some peas in the kitchen when her phone screen flashed with a call. Wiping her hands on her apron, she leaned over to pick up her daughter's call.

"Mom, I have to tell you something," Tashi gushed.

"Even I have to tell you something," she smiled.

"I got a promotion and a raise," she squealed in joy, without letting her mother finish.

"That is such good news. I am so happy for you, Ashi dear."

"Let's celebrate by taking a trip to Shimla – just you and I."

"I would love that," her mother laughed. "Are you sure you don't want to bring Venkat along?"

"Mom!" she chided, blushing. "Venkat is just a friend; you know that."

"Yeah, and who are you going out for dinner and drinks tonight?"

"Mom, stop pulling my leg. Tell me, what were you about to say?"

"Manav called. He said he is back in town for a few days."

"Aww, he called you? That is so sweet. I know he is in Delhi. In fact, Venkat and I are meeting Manav and his fiancée in the evening. Also, I have booked our tickets to Shimla for tonight."

"Okay, dear. But," she said, her voice losing the laughter. "Are you sure a trip is a good idea right now? I mean..."

"Mom," Tashi stopped her mid-sentence. "I have thought about it long enough. I am ready for a holiday."

"But Dr Prasad said – "

"The counsellor said my heart knows what's best for me better than any medicines or therapy sessions. And right now, every particle in my body is screaming that a change of scenery is exactly what I need."

"I am happy you feel that way. But what if-"

"What if, what, mom? You're worried I might get another anxiety attack on being surrounded by so many strangers?"

"I didn't mean that, dear," her mother blurted.

"I have been working on myself, mom. For months after the blackmailer was caught, I felt as if there was a volcano inside my chest, flaming with heat each time I took a breath. But it has subsided, the fear is gone. This is the most confident I have felt since then. I'll be fine – I cannot live in terror all my life, can I? You get busy packing. Take all the woollens you might need and a big bag for we will do lots of shopping."

"Okay dear," her mother replied with a sigh. "Take care."

"I will, mom. And this weekend, you and I are going to have a blast."

***

If you stay silent now,

years down the line

when you find enough courage,

the world is not going to believe

your pain was real.

Why, they will ask,

did you let the demon breathe?

Why did you let it take the fire from your soul

and breathe it down your body?

They will see your bruises,

the broken bones,

the scars all over your fair skin,

and even then, they will say

that somehow,
in some twisted, inhuman way,

all of it was your fault.

Don't believe them.

You are the one who lived through it.

They didn't.

It is easy to criticise a home

someone else has built.

It is crushing

to put your blood and sweat

into building one,

watch it die in front of your eyes,

and still, bring out courage
from the depths of your soul-

courage to hope that,

somehow,

it would survive.

Yes, you were late in admitting the hurt

but being late doesn't mean you were wrong.

Darling, this wasn't your fault.

About The Author

A two-time Quora Top Writer and top writer in fiction on Medium, Anangsha specializes in poetry and short fiction. Her compositions have won several national and international awards. Her poetry debut Stolen Reflections ended up as an Amazon bestseller within four days of its release and is still going strong on the Amazon Bestsellers list.

Apart from her writing career, Anangsha holds a masters degree in civil engineering from IIT Guwahati. She is currently pursuing her Ph.D. part-time while working as an Assistant Professor at NIT Silchar. She hopes to write her own fantasy fiction series someday.

Note From The Author

My Facebook account was hacked in 2016.

For about two weeks, an anonymous stranger on the internet had access to every post I had shared over the last six years of being active on social media. He could read every message I had sent, go through every desperate 3 AM-call-for-help to my nearest ones. He could see the photographs I had shared with my boyfriend over the one year or so we spent in a long distance relationship.

Basically, someone gained access to a large chunk of my online life without me ever letting him in. It was akin to a stranger entering your home and looking through your personal documents and photographs without your consent.

And it was terrifying.

Soul-crushing, self-esteem shattering.

I had to pull some strings to gain access back into my account. But two weeks is a long time. He could have already made a backup of my files somewhere.

I got my Facebook account back, but the hacker was never caught. And it makes my breath catch in my throat every time I think that someone out there in the world has seen me at my most vulnerable.

To be honest, even now, three years down the line, I sometimes worry about what would happen if he chooses to release all the photographs and videos online.

This incident changed me as a person. It made me realise how easy it is to be a victim of cybercrime, and how much effect threats like these have on a woman's emotional and mental wellbeing.

This was when Tashi's story started to dig roots in the deepest pits of my consciousness. I knew I had to share my story, my pain, and trauma with the world; and a fiction novella was the best way to do so.

And thus, the story for "What did Tashi do?" was born.

www.ingramcontent.com/pod-product-compliance
Lightning Source LLC
LaVergne TN
LVHW041848070526
838199LV00045BA/1490